OUT OF THIS WORLD

SCIENCE FICTION STORIES

KINGFISHER

First published as *Science Fiction Stories* 1988 by Kingfisher
This edition first published 2008 by Kingfisher
an imprint of Macmillan Children's Books
a division of Macmillan Publishers Limited
20 New Wharf Road, London N1 9RR
Basingstoke and Oxford
Associated companies throughout the world
www.panmacmillan.com

ISBN: 978-0-7534-1633-4

This selection copyright © Edward Blishen 1988, 1991
The acknowledgements on page 272 constitute an extension of the copyright page.

The moral right of the compiler and authors has been asserted.

1 3 5 7 9 10 8 6 4 2
1TR/0508/PROSP/(MA)/80NP/C

A CIP catalogue record for this book is available from the British Library.

Printed in China

OUT OF THIS WORLD

SCIENCE FICTION STORIES

Chosen by Edward Blishen

KINGFISHER

CONTENTS

The Boy, the Dog and the Spaceship

Nicholas Fisk

THERE WAS A boy and his dog, running and rolling and chasing in a field.

There was a spaceship hurtling through nothingness, most of its crew already dead, and the rest despairingly fighting on to make landfall on a strange planet.

The boy's name was Billy. He was nine. His dog was called Scamp. He was young too. Boy and dog understood each other perfectly.

Billy shouted, "Devil dog!" and pounced at Scamp. Scamp rolled his eyes, yelped with delight and pranced off sideways. Billy chased Scamp until he was tired out. Then they sat down together, side by side in the evening shadows. When they had got their breath back, Billy shouted, "Devil dog!" and the chase started all over again.

In the spaceship, the Captain contacted the Engineer. The channel was live – the Captain could hear the slight echoing hiss from the speaker. Or was it the Engineer's laboured breathing?

The Captain barked, "Report. I want your report. Make your report."

The Engineer's breathing changed. It turned into long sobs. "*Report.*"

The Engineer spoke. "It's no good, Captain, it's no good . . .! The heat's burned out the bounce beam, the retros have gone dead. We'll just hit, Captain. We're going to smash."

Seconds later, the retros bellowed and the ship checked so violently that the Captain fell over. He got up bleeding. He said, "Engineer!" then noticed the Engineer's light had died which meant that the Engineer had died. So he called the In-Flight Tech.

"In-Flight, we have full retro, am I correct?"

"Eighty per cent retro, Captain. No more to come. But it may be enough –"

"It must be enough."

"Yes, Captain."

"Very well. Crashball, In-Flight. And tell the others."

"The others," the Captain said to himself. "Just two others . . ."

He switched off and began to fit himself into the crashball cocoon. He fitted webbing harnesses over his body and buckled them. He pressed a button and padded arms enfolded him. A little tubular snake leapt from a padded hole and latched itself to a socket near his neck; his clothing began to swell, then the walls of the cocoon. The puffed surfaces met. Now he was completely encased in a puffy softness, pressing tighter and tighter.

He waited for the stab. It came. The needle darted itself into one of the Captain's veins. A drug entered his bloodstream.

Almost immediately he felt drowsy and comfortable, but still alert. The same needle was connected to a whole junction of tiny tubes filled with his own blood and plasma; with stimulants, pain-killers, curatives and other life givers and life adjusters; even with painless death.

"Check in," said the Captain.

The In-Flight Tech and the Coordinator should have answered. Their lights were live. The Coordinator said, "Excuse me, Captain, but I think I'm dying." A moment later he died.

"In-Flight Tech," said the Captain.

No answer.

"In-Flight Tech! Check in!"

"Yes, Captain?"

"Just checking," said the Captain, and switched off so that the Tech should not hear his sigh of relief.

The ship hurtled on. It was still slowing, the Captain could feel it through the cocoon. In the control centre, the screens showed a green and blue planet with seas and clouds and land masses, coming nearer all the time. But there was no one outside the cocoons to watch the screens.

The boy whistled for his dog. "Here boy!" he commanded, and whistled again. "Come on, Scamp!"

Scamp pranced and curvetted towards the boy, being silly. He wanted to make the boy laugh, but the boy was solemn. He was proud of having such a well-trained dog. "Good boy," he said gravely. "Good old Scamp."

A minute later, the boy and the dog were wrestling in the grass.

The ship entered Earth's atmosphere. Its metal skin now drove against air instead of nothingness. The ship screamed. Its metal skin changed colour and in places glowed dull red with the heat.

The In-Flight Tech's cocoon shifted, tearing from its framing. A cluster of tiny tubes pulled away from a socket, away from the needle. Blood, drugs, squirted uselessly. The In-Flight Tech died without a word.

The Captain watched his light go out and said, "All right. All right. Alone. I'll do it alone."

They stopped their wrestling match and looked about them.

"You heard it! It went sort of *wheeoosh*," Billy said to Scamp. "*Wheeeeeooooosh.*" Scamp flicked his head sideways to acknowledge his master's words, but went on staring at the dark corner of the trees. Scamp had heard the noise. He didn't know where it came from, but he knew where it led. He marked the place in his nose and mind. Over there, by the dark trees.

"So that's what it's like," said the Captain. He had never before experienced a smash landing. He had to say something, even if there was no one to hear him. He kept his voice level.

He waited for the needle to deliver whatever his body needed. While he waited, he disciplined his mind and made it think and plan.

"Conquest," his mind said. "I am alone, but I am still here as a conqueror. I will conquer this planet.

"Method," he continued. "I am alone; but usual procedure

10

will be followed. I will find a creature of the planet. I will invade its mind: make it obey me. I will then make all creatures of its kind obey the creature I inhabit.

"Having conquered one creature and one species, I will move on, always seeking the higher creatures. If there is a ruling species on this planet, I will invade a creature of that species and thus become ruler of all."

He pressed the release control. The halves of the cocoon opened.

The new conqueror of the planet Earth flexed his limbs, tested his organs and senses, opened the main doors and stepped forth.

Billy pretended not to hear his mother's call, but then decided to obey. A long way away, right at the edge of the field, he could see the yellow glimmer of the lamp on her bicycle. "Oh lor," he thought, "she's had to get on the bike to come after me. She won't be pleased . . ." To the dog he said, "Come on, Scamp. Come on, boy!" But Scamp was running back and forth by the dark trees.

"Bill-eeeee!" his mother shouted. "You come home now, or I'll —"

"It's Scamp, *he* won't come!" shouted Billy furiously.

And he wouldn't. Billy could see Scamp running up and down, doing a sort of sentry duty on the trot by the edge of the trees. The dog's ears were pricked, his tail was high, his body alert. He wouldn't obey.

The Captain's helmet indicators read SAFE, so the planet's air was breathable. Nevertheless, he kept his helmet on. He was glad to be protected with helmet and armour. He was grateful to the brains and skills that had designed his armoured suit and given him a strength greater than his own. The Captain would clench a hand – and the suit's own metal hand would clench with such force that it could crush metal. The Captain was strong and fit – but his suit was tireless and inexhaustible. If the Captain's nerves, muscles and movements said "run", the suit would run endlessly. If the Captain's body said "climb", the suit would keep climbing for him.

Now was the time, the Captain realized, to climb.

He had seen many worlds, explored many planets. He had never seen one like this. This world was bursting with life. From the corner of his eye, the Captain saw something move, very fast, on several legs. Above him, something flew. Behind him, something scurried. He was not in the least surprised. How could there fail to be active, animal life in so rich a place?

Climbing was what mattered now. He had to get on and up. Where he stood, he was completely surrounded and blinded by vegetable richness. Great green ribbed things, taller than the highest mountains of his own planet, reached indefinitely upwards – no, not indefinitely, he could see dark blue sky still further above. A vast green trunk sprang from the soil very near him. It was the right size and shape and it had projections: ideal for climbing. He clasped his limbs round this trunk. The suit took over and climbed him towards the dark blue sky, away from the ship with its hideous cargo of broken bodies; and from the stench of death.

At first there had just been a faint whiff of it. Now, it was a full-bodied and glorious stench – better still, a new stench! Scamp's black nostrils widened still further. There! Over there! He gave a stifled yelp of ecstasy as the smell strengthened; he bounded towards it.

"Billy!" said his mother. "Never mind the dog, you come home and eat your supper. Come on, now! I'm not waiting a moment longer!"

Billy stopped and gave one last yell. "Scamp! Scaaaaamp!"

Scamp did not hear. Only tracking down the smell mattered.

The Captain could climb no higher. The green column that supported him was bending and swaying under his weight. He wrapped his limbs round the column and felt the suit lock itself securely into position. He looked around him.

He was in a dense forest of green columns, all very much the same as the one he had climbed yet each different. A few were rod-like (his column was ribbed and almost flat). Some columns carried grotesque explosions of strange branching shapes on their heads. A great nest of columns in the distance supported flat, outward-branching green platforms and – amazing! – complicated crown-shaped yellow platforms at their summits.

He adjusted his helmet to take in air from the outside. The air was moist, perfumed, sumptuous. He let the helmet supply his mouth with a sample of the moisture that was making droplets over everything; the water was cold, clean, simple, almost certainly safe – and absolutely delicious. On his own planet, he had tasted such air and water only in laboratories. Reluctantly, he returned to the closed-circuit environment of his suit and helmet . . .

An amazing planet! A planet of limitless, unending, inexhaustible richness! And he was to be its conqueror. The thought was stunning. For once, the Captain allowed himself simply to feel pleasure: to stare at nothing and to dream of glory.

Here! Scamp's nose was actually touching the wonderful source of the supreme stench!

He licked the source of the smell. It was cold and dewy and hard. He had expected something still warm, still half alive, still rubbery-soft; it was that sort of smell. But perhaps the cold, hard outer case was only a container, like the tube of bone that encloses the marrow? Carefully, he opened his mouth and picked up the container thing in his jaws. Nothing happened, so he put it down again, holding it between his front paws, and looked at it with his head on one side.

It seemed harmless. He lowered his head, opened his jaws and bit.

The Captain saw a monster.

Once the terror and shock were over there were three things to be done (Past, Present and Future, as the training manuals put it). First, understand exactly what had happened

– the Past; second, make up your mind what immediate action to take – Present; third, decide what advantage could be gained by further action – Future.

All right. Past. He had seen the monster – a living thing, not a machine – travel at incredible speed, crash through the green columns and spires, trampling them flat in its haste. The monster was white, brown and black and ran on legs. It had made straight for the crashed ship. When the monster's face opened, it was pink inside and had pointed white mountains above and below.

The monster had done various things that the Captain could not see to the ship. Finally it had picked up the ship, holding it between the white mountains, and crushed it. The Captain had heard the metal screech.

All right. Now the Present.

The body of the monster must be entered by the Captain so that the Captain could take it over in the usual way. He had to get nearer the monster. That should be easy enough provided that the monster did not suddenly go away on its big legs.

Finally, the Future.

Well, that was obvious enough, thought the Captain. Follow the normal procedure. Invade the monster's brain and gain control of its body and its actions.

After that, the invasion would follow its normal course. All species – high or low – would eventually obey the Captain. By then the Captain would have contacted his home planet. More ships would come bearing settlers. At last the Captain's race would have found a safe, fitting, rich and permanent home.

He went towards the monster.

Billy picked at his supper, but his mother said, "Do eat up!" and watched him until he finished every morsel. He didn't want food. He wanted Scamp.

His mother said, "And do your homework." She bustled out of the room. A minute or so later he heard the TV. She liked that programme, she never missed it! And she wouldn't miss *him*.

He tiptoed to the back door, opened it silently, closed it silently, and was on his way to the big field.

The Captain was within reach. The white parts of the monster glowed pale but clear in the failing light. The Captain muttered, "Climb". The suit took him up fast.

The Captain had chosen a green spire to climb – a flat-sided spire that would bend when he reached the top of it. The monster was not moving. It was crouched over the remains of the ship. "Climb. Climb . . ."

Just as he reached the right place and was about to sway the tip of his spire towards the monster, the monster moved! The Captain made a split-second decision and leaped into nothingness. He stretched his limbs – clutched – and held. Victory!

Gripping one cluster of white or brown or black rods after another, the Captain clambered his way along the monster, making for the brain. It was above the monster's face. He could feel the brain's energy.

He came to the entrance of a tunnel leading into the monster's head and smiled. He clambered into the tunnel, the suit making light work of the journey. Now the brain signals were deafening – even the helmet was overwhelmed. The Captain turned back. He made himself comfortable outside the entrance of the tunnel, anchoring himself securely. He checked some readings and responses. Good. The monster was hearing him.

"You'll enjoy this," the Captain told the monster. "You'll like obeying me. You'll like the things we do. You *will* obey me, won't you? Of course you will. You *will* obey me, always . . ."

Billy found Scamp. At first he was glad to find him, but soon he was puzzled. Scamp kept shaking his head, and he was running. "He's got a burr in his ear," thought Billy. "Or an insect. An itch."

Scamp was running in regular patterns – a straight line, a pause, a turn to the left, then another straight line, then a pause and a turn to the right. It looked weird in the moonlight. Billy began to be frightened.

Then Scamp suddenly sat down, some ten yards away, and looked straight at Billy. The dog did not move a muscle. He just stared.

The Captain halted the monster – the up-and-down motion of the monster's running disturbed his thought – and thought very carefully.

"The monster is a servant creature," he decided. "And the upright monster, the one that just arrived, is a superior creature because he makes audio signals and expects them to be obeyed. How do I know that? Because when the upright monster made his signals, my monster was uneasy. He tried to disobey me." The Captain smiled a little at the thought.

"But does it matter which monster is the master?" he thought. Probably not. They are both much the same size. If they fought who knows which would win?

"Not that *that* matters much either," thought the Captain. "Because I am the controlling brain. So I could appoint either as the master species of the planet. Nevertheless . . ."

Billy shouted, "Scamp! Come here when I call you!" But Scamp just sat there in the moonlight, staring straight at him, motionless.

Billy said – this time almost pleading – "Come on, boy. Good boy. Come on, Scamp. Please."

But the dog just stared and his eyes looked strange in the moonlight.

"Nevertheless," thought the Captain, "it might be as well to find out which is master. Besides, one or other of them might have powerful weapons I should know about. I'll try it."

He spoke to the dog's brain.

"Kill," said the Captain. "Kill that other creature there."

The dog attacked. "Scamp!" yelled Billy. "Don't, Scamp!"

Scamp overran him and turned and charged again, snarling like a hound of hell. And then the dog had hurtled the boy to the ground and was standing over him, jaws open, teeth bared.

"*Scamp!*" It was a scream of terror. The dog paused. The big voice in his head said, "*Kill!*" but the old, loved, familiar voice was calling too, asking for help.

The dog paused; the boy struck out blindly with his fist. He hit the dog's ear. Something small fell to the ground unseen. The little thing was mortally wounded. It writhed.

Scamp said, "Whoof!" in a vague way and looked at Billy. The dog licked the boy's face, wagged his tail and sheepishly got off Billy's chest. He sat down and scratched his ear with a hind paw. But the itching had gone.

The little, unseen thing writhed for the last time; and, hidden in the grass, the Captain died.

The boy and the dog rollicked off together across the moonlit field. Sometimes the boy chased the dog: sometimes the dog chased the boy. When they got home, they were both scolded by Billy's mother.

By the edge of the trees, the dew was heavy on the spaceship. Soon it would rust and become as brown as the earth. But now it was still shiny and glinting in the tall weeds. In the moonlight, you wouldn't have noticed where its body was crushed and dented. It looked like a super-perfect model. Little, but marvellously made.

INVISIBLE IN LONDON

FROM *THE INVISIBLE MAN*

H. G. WELLS

*How wonderful to be invisible! What one could do! How
powerful one would be, moving about unseen!
The scientist in this story has discovered the secret of
invisibility. Undressed (because he couldn't make his clothes
invisible) he walks out into the wintry streets of London, full
of excitement and expectation . . .*

"IN GOING DOWNSTAIRS the first time I found an
unexpected difficulty because I could not see my feet; indeed
I stumbled twice, and there was an unaccustomed clumsiness
in gripping the bolt. By not looking down, however, I
managed to walk on the level passably well.

"My mood, I saw, was one of exaltation. I felt as a seeing
man might do, with padded feet and noiseless clothes, in a city
of the blind. I experienced a wild impulse to jest, to startle
people, to clap men on the back, fling people's hats astray, and
generally revel in my extraordinary advantage.

"But hardly had I emerged upon Great Portland Street,
however (my lodging was close to the big draper's shop there),
when I heard a clashing concussion and was hit violently

behind, and turning saw a man carrying a basket of soda-water syphons, and looking in amazement at his burden. Although the blow had really hurt me, I found something so irresistible in his astonishment that I laughed aloud. 'The devil's in the basket,' I said, and suddenly twisted it out of his hand. He let it go incontinently, and I swung the whole weight into the air.

"But a fool of a cabman, standing outside a public house, made a sudden rush for this, and his extending fingers took me with excruciating violence under the ear. I let the whole down with a smash on the cabman, and then, with shouts and the clatter of feet about me, people coming out of the shops, vehicles pulling up, I realized what I had done for myself, and cursing my folly, backed against a shop window and prepared to dodge out of the confusion. In a moment I should be wedged into a crowd and inevitably discovered. I pushed by the butcher boy, who luckily did not turn to see the nothingness that shoved him aside, and dodged behind the cabman's four-wheeler. I do not know how they settled the business. I hurried straight across the road, which was happily clear, and hardly heeding which way I went, in the fright of detection the incident had given, plunged into the afternoon throng of Oxford Street.

"I tried to get into the stream of people, but they were too thick for me, and in a moment my heels were being trodden upon. I took to the gutter, the roughness of which I found painful to my feet, and forthwith the shaft of a crawling hansom dug me forcibly under the shoulder blade, reminding me that I was already bruised severely. I staggered out of the way of the cab, avoided a perambulator by a convulsive movement, and found myself behind the hansom. A happy thought saved me, and as this drove slowly along I followed in its immediate wake, trembling and astonished at the turn of my adventure. And not only trembling, but shivering. It was a bright day in January and I was stark naked and the thin slime of mud that covered the road was freezing. Foolish as it seems to me now, I had not reckoned that, transparent or not, I was still amenable to the weather and all its consequences.

"Then suddenly a bright idea came into my head. I ran round and got into the cab. And so, shivering, scared, and sniffing with the first intimations of a cold, and with the bruises in the small of my back growing upon my attention, I drove slowly along Oxford Street and past Tottenham Court Road. My mood was as different from that in which I had sallied forth ten minutes ago as it is possible to imagine. *This* invisibility indeed! The one thought that possessed me was – how was I to get out of the scrape I was in.

"We crawled past Mudie's, and there a tall woman with five or six yellow-labelled books hailed my cab, and I sprang out just in time to escape her, shaving a railway van narrowly in my flight. I made off up the roadway to Bloomsbury Square, intending to strike north past the Museum and so get into the quiet district. I was now cruelly chilled, and the strangeness of my situation so unnerved me that I whimpered as I ran. At the northward corner of the square a little white dog ran out of the Pharmaceutical Society's offices, and incontinently made for me, nose down.

"I had never realized it before, but the nose is to the mind of a dog what the eye is to the mind of a seeing man. Dogs perceive the scent of a man moving as men perceive his vision. This brute began barking and leaping, showing, as it seemed to me, only too plainly that he was aware of me. I crossed Great Russell Street, glancing over my shoulder as I did so, and went some way along Montagu Street before I realized what I was running towards.

"Then I became aware of a blare of music, and looking along the street saw a number of people advancing out of Russell Square, red shirts, and the banner of the Salvation Army to the fore. Such a crowd, chanting in the roadway and scoffing on the pavement, I could not hope to penetrate, and dreading to go back and farther from home again, and deciding on the spur of the moment, I ran up the white steps of a house facing the museum railings, and stood there until the crowd should have passed. Happily the dog stopped at the noise of the band too, hesitated, and turned tail, running back to Bloomsbury Square again.

"On came the band, bawling with unconscious irony some hymn about 'When shall we see his Face?' and it seemed an interminable time to me before the tide of the crowd washed along the pavement by me. Thud, thud, thud came the drum with a vibrating resonance, and for the moment I did not notice two urchins stopping at the railings by me. 'See 'em?' said one. 'See what?' said the other. 'Why – them footmarks – *bare*. Like what you makes in mud.'

"I looked down and saw the youngsters had stopped and

were gaping at the muddy footmarks I had left behind me up the newly whitened steps. The passing people elbowed and jostled them, but their confounded intelligence was arrested. 'Thud, thud, thud, When, thud, shall we see, thud, his face, thud, thud.' 'There's a barefoot man gone up them steps, or I don't know nothing,' said one. 'And he ain't never come down again. And his foot was a-bleeding.'

"The thick of the crowd had already passed. 'Looky there, Ted,' quoth the younger of the detectives, with the sharpness of surprise in his voice, and pointed straight to my feet. I looked down and saw at once the dim suggestion of their outline sketched in splashes of mud. For a moment I was paralyzed.

"'Why, that's rum,' said the elder. 'Dashed rum! It's just like the ghost of a foot, ain't it?' He hesitated and advanced with outstretched hand. A man pulled up short to see what he was catching, and then a girl. In another moment he would have touched me. Then I saw what to do. I made a step, the boy started back with an exclamation, and with a rapid movement I swung myself over into the portico of the next house, but the smaller boy was sharp-eyed enough to follow the movement, and before I was well down the steps and upon the pavement, he had recovered from his momentary astonishment and was shouting out that the feet had gone over the wall.

"They rushed round and saw my new footmarks flash into being on the lower step and upon the pavement. 'What's up?' asked someone. 'Feet! Look! Feet running!' Everybody in the road, except my three pursuers, was pouring along after the

Salvation Army, and this not only impeded me but them. There was an eddy of surprise and interrogation. At the cost of bowling over one young fellow I got through, and in another moment I was rushing headlong round the circuit of Russell Square, with six or seven astonished people following my footmarks. There was no time for explanation, or else the whole host would have been after me.

"Twice I doubled round corners, thrice I crossed the road and came back on my tracks, and then, as my feet grew hot and dry, the damp impressions began to fade. At last I had a breathing space and rubbed my feet clean with my hands, and so got away altogether. The last I saw of the chase was a little group of a dozen people perhaps, studying with infinite perplexity a slowly drying footprint that had resulted from a puddle in Tavistock Square – a footprint as isolated and incomprehensible to them as Crusoe's solitary discovery.

"This running warmed me to a certain extent, and I went on with a better courage through the maze of less frequented roads that runs hereabouts. My back had now become very stiff and sore, my tonsils were painful from the cabman's fingers, and the skin of my neck had been scratched by his nails; my feet hurt exceedingly and I was lame from a little cut on my foot. I saw in time a blind man approaching me, and fled limping, for I feared his subtle intuitions. Once or twice accidental collisions occurred and I left people amazed, with unaccountable curses ringing in their ears. Then came something silent and quiet against my face, and across the Square fell a thin veil of slowly falling flakes of snow. I had caught a cold, and do as I would I could not avoid an occasional sneeze. And every dog that came in sight, with its pointing nose and curious sniffing, was a terror to me.

"Then came men and boys running, first one and then others, and shouting as they ran. It was a fire. They ran in the direction of my lodging, and looking back down a street I saw a mass of black smoke streaming up above the roofs and telephone wires. It was my lodging burning; my clothes, my apparatus, all my resources indeed, except my cheque-book and the three books of memoranda that awaited me in Great Portland Street, were there. Burning! I had burnt my boats – if ever a man did!"

THE DRAGON OF PENDOR

FROM *A WIZARD OF EARTHSEA*

URSULA LE GUIN

Ged, or Sparrowhawk, is a young mage, or wizard, who has been trained in magic, and has turned out to be more gifted than it's good even for the most brilliant wizard to be. Answering a dangerous challenge he has called a spirit back from the dead, and now — having done what no one should do — is himself pursued by a terrible black shadow. He is sent to an island to work magic for the people and to rid them of dragons that prey upon them. He finds the black shadow is still pursuing him there, and preventing him from working his necessary, good magic on behalf of the islanders. There is only one thing to do.

THE NEXT MORNING he went down among the fishermen in the principal moorage of Low Torning, and finding the Head Isle-Man there said to him, "I must leave this place. I am in danger, and I put you in danger. I must go. Therefore I ask your leave to go out and do away with the dragons on Pendor, so that my task for you will be finished and I may leave freely. Or if I fail, I should fail also when they come here, and that is better known now than later."

The Isle-Man stared at him all dropjawed. "Lord Sparrowhawk," he said, "there are nine dragons out there!"

"Eight are still young, they say."

"But the old one –"

"I tell you, I must go from here. I ask your leave to rid you of the dragon-peril first, if I can do so."

"As you will, Sir," the Isle-Man said gloomily. All that listened there thought this a folly or a crazy courage in their young wizard, and with sullen faces they saw him go, expecting no news of him again. Some hinted that he meant merely to sail back by Hosk to the Inmost Sea, leaving them in the lurch; others, among the Pechvarry, held that he had gone mad, and sought death.

For four generations of men all ships had set their course to keep far from the shores of Pendor Island. No mage had ever come to do combat with the dragon there, for the island was on no travelled sea-road, and its lords had been pirates, slave-takers, war-makers, hated by all that dwelt in the southwest parts of Earthsea. For this reason none had sought to revenge the Lord of Pendor, after the dragon came suddenly out of the west upon him and his men where they sat feasting in the tower, and smothered them with the flames of his mouth, and drove all the townsfolk screaming into the sea. Unavenged, Pendor had been left to the dragon, with all its bones, and towers, and jewels stolen from long-dead princes of the coasts of Paln and Hosk.

All this Ged knew well, and more, for ever since he came to Low Torning he had held in mind and pondered over all he had ever learned of dragons. As he guided his small boat westward – not rowing now nor using the seaman's skill Pechvarry had taught him, but sailing wizardly with the magewind in his sail and a spell set on prow and keel to keep them true – he watched to see the dead isle rise on the rim of the sea. Speed he wanted, and therefore used the magewind, for he feared what was behind him more than what was before him. But as the day passed, his impatience turned from fear to a kind of glad fierceness. At least he sought this danger of his own will; and the nearer he came to it the more sure he was that, for this time at least, for this hour perhaps before his death, he was free. The shadow dared not follow him into the dragon's jaws. The waves ran white-tipped on the grey sea, and grey clouds streamed overhead on the north wind. He went west with the quick magewind in his sail, and came in sight of the rocks of Pendor, the still streets of the town, and the gutted, falling towers.

At the entrance of the harbour, a shallow crescent bay, he let the windspell drop and stilled his little boat so it lay rocking on the waves. Then he summoned the dragon: "Usurper of Pendor, come defend your hoard!"

His voice fell short in the sound of breakers beating on the ashen shores; but dragons have keen ears. Presently one flitted up from some roofless ruin of the town like a vast black bat, thin-winged and spiny-backed, and circling into the north wind came flying towards Ged. His heart swelled at the sight of the creature that was a myth to his people, and he laughed and shouted, "Go tell the Old One to come, you wind-worm!"

For this was one of the young dragons, spawned there years ago by a she-dragon from the West Reach, who had set her clutch of great leathern eggs, as they say she-dragons will, in some sunny broken room of the tower and had flown away again, leaving the Old Dragon of Pendor to watch the young when they crawled like baneful lizards from the shell.

The young dragon made no answer. He was not large of his kind, maybe the length of a forty-oared ship, and was worm-thin for all the reach of his black membranous wings. He had not got his growth yet, nor his voice, nor any dragon-cunning. Straight at Ged in the small rocking boat he came, opening his long, toothed jaws as he slid down arrowy from the air: so that all Ged had to do was bind his wings and limbs stiff with one sharp spell and send him thus hurtling aside into the sea like a stone falling. And the grey sea closed over him.

Two dragons like the first rose up from the base of the highest tower. Even as the first one they came driving straight at Ged, and even so he caught both, hurled both down, and drowned them; and he had not yet lifted up his wizard's staff.

Now after a little time there came three against him from the island. One of those was much greater, and fire spewed curling from its jaws. Two came flying at him rattling their wings, but the big one came circling from behind, very swift, to burn him and his boat with its breath of fire. No binding spell would catch all three, because two came from north and one from south. In the instant that he saw this, Ged worked a spell of Changing, and between one breath and the next flew up from his boat in dragon-form.

Spreading broad wings and reaching talons out, he met the two head on, withering them with fire, and then turned to the third, who was larger than he and armed also with fire. On the wind over the grey waves they doubled, snapped, swooped, lunged, till smoke roiled about them red-lit by the glare of their fiery mouths. Ged flew suddenly upward and the other pursued, below him. In midflight the dragon-Ged raised wings, stopped, and stooped as the hawk stoops, talons outstretched downwards, striking and bearing the other down by neck and flank. The black wings flurried and black dragon-blood dropped in thick drops into the sea. The Pendor dragon tore free and flew low and lamely to the island, where it hid, crawling into some well or cavern in the ruined town.

At once Ged took his form and place again on the boat, for it was most perilous to keep that dragon-shape longer than need demanded. His hands were black with the scalding wormblood, and he was scorched about the head with fire, but this was no matter now. He waited only till he had his breath back and then called, "Six I have seen, five slain, nine are told of: come out, worms!"

No creature moved nor voice spoke for a long while on the island, but only the waves beat loudly on the shore. Then Ged was aware that the highest tower slowly changed its shape, bulging out on one side as if it grew an arm. He feared dragon-magic, for old dragons are very powerful and guileful in a sorcery like and unlike the sorcery of men: but a moment more and he saw this was no trick of the dragon, but of his own eyes. What he had taken for a part of the tower was the shoulder of the Dragon Pendor as he uncurled his bulk and lifted himself slowly up.

When he was all afoot his scaled head, spike-crowned and triple-tongued, rose higher than the broken tower's height, and his taloned forefeet rested on the rubble of the town below. His scales were grey-black, catching the daylight like broken stone. Lean as a hound he was and huge as a hill. Ged stared in awe. There was no song or tale could prepare the mind for this sight. Almost he stared into the dragon's eyes and was caught, for one cannot look into a dragon's eyes. He glanced away from the oily green gaze that watched him, and held up before him his staff, that looked now like a splinter, like a twig.

"Eight sons I had, little wizard," said the great dry voice of the dragon. "Five died, one dies: enough. You will not win my hoard by killing them."

"I do not want your hoard."

The yellow smoke hissed from the dragon's nostrils: that was his laughter.

"Would you not like to come ashore and look at it, little wizard? It is worth looking at."

"No, dragon." The kinship of dragons is with wind and fire, and they do not fight willingly over the sea. That had been Ged's advantage so far and he kept it; but the strip of seawater between him and the great grey talons did not seem much of an advantage, any more.

It was hard not to look into the green, watching eyes.

"You are a very young wizard," the dragon said. "I did not

know men came so young into their power." He spoke, as did Ged, in the Old Speech, for that is the tongue of dragons still. Although the use of the Old Speech binds a man to truth, this is not so with dragons. It is their own language and they can lie in it, twisting the true words to false ends, catching the unwary hearer in a maze of mirror-words each of which reflects the truth and none of which leads anywhere. So Ged had been warned often, and when the dragon spoke he listened with an untrustful ear, all his doubts ready. But the words seemed plain and clear: "Is it to ask my help that you have come here, little wizard?"

"No, dragon."

"Yet I could help you. You will need help soon, against that which hunts you in the dark."

Ged stood dumb.

"What is it that hunts you? Name it to me."

"If I could name it – " Ged stopped himself.

Yellow smoke curled above the dragon's long head, from the nostrils that were two round pits of fire.

"If you could name it you could master it, maybe, little wizard. Maybe I could tell you its name, when I see it close by. And it will come close, if you wait about my isle. It will come wherever you come. If you do not want it to come close you must run, and run, and keep running from it. And yet it will follow you. Would you like to know its name?"

Ged stood silent again. How the dragon knew of the shadow he had loosed, he could not guess, nor how it might know the shadow's name. The Archmage had said that the

33

shadow had no name. Yet dragons have their own wisdom; and they are an older race than man. Few men could guess what a dragon knows and how he knows it, and those few are the Dragonlords. To Ged, only one thing was sure: that, though the dragon might well be speaking truth, though he might indeed be able to tell Ged the nature and name of the shadow-thing and so give him power over it – even so, even if he spoke truth, he did so wholly for his own ends.

"It is very seldom," the young man said at last, "that dragons ask to do men favours."

"But it is very common," said the dragon, "for cats to play with mice before they kill them."

"But I did not come here to play, or to be played with. I came to strike a bargain with you."

Like a sword in sharpness but five times the length of any sword, the point of the dragon's tail arched up scorpionwise over his mailed back, above the tower. Dryly he spoke: "I strike no bargain. I take. What have you to offer that I cannot take from you when I like?"

"Safety. Your safety. Swear that you will never fly eastward of Pendor, and I will swear to leave you unharmed."

A grating sound came from the dragon's throat like the noise of an avalanche far off, stones falling among mountains. Fire danced along his three-forked tongue. He raised himself up higher, looming over the ruins. "You offer me safety! You threaten me! With what?"

"With your name, Yevaud."

Ged's voice shook as he spoke the name, yet he spoke it

clear and loud. At the sound of it, the old dragon held still, utterly still. A minute went by, and another; and then Ged, standing there in his rocking chip of a boat, smiled. He had staked this venture and his life on a guess drawn from old histories of dragon-lore learned on Roke, a guess that this Dragon of Pendor was the same that had spoiled the west of Osskil in the days of Elfarran and Morred, and had been driven from Osskil by a wizard, Elt, wise in names. The guess had held.

"We are matched, Yevaud. You have your strength: I have your name. Will you bargain?"

Still the dragon made no reply.

Many years had the dragon sprawled on the island where golden breastplates and emeralds lay scattered among dust and bricks and bones; he had watched his black lizard-brood play among crumbling houses and try their wings from the cliffs; he had slept long in the sun, unawakened by voice or sail. He had grown old. It was hard now to stir, to face this magelad, this frail enemy, at the sight of whose staff Yevaud, the old dragon, winced.

"You may choose nine stones from my hoard," he said at last, his voice hissing and whining in his long jaws. "The best: take your choice. Then go!"

"I do not want your stones, Yevaud."

"Where is men's greed gone? Men loved bright stones in the old days in the North . . . I know not what it is you want, wizard. I, too, can offer you safety, for I know what can save you. I know what alone can save you. There is a horror follows you. I will tell you its name."

35

Ged's heart leaped in him, and he clutched his staff, standing as still as the dragon stood. He fought a moment with sudden, startling hope.

It was not his own life that he bargained for. One mastery, and only one, could he hold over the dragon. He set hope aside and did what he must do.

"That is not what I ask for, Yevaud."

When he spoke the dragon's name it was as if he held the huge being on a fine, thin leash, tightening it on his throat. He could feel the ancient malice and experience of men in the dragon's gaze that rested on him, he could see the steel talons each as long as a man's forearm, and the stone-hard hide, and the withering fire that lurked in the dragon's throat: and yet always the leash tightened, tightened.

He spoke again: "Yevaud! Swear by your name that you and your sons will never come to the Archipelago."

Flames broke suddenly bright and loud from the dragon's jaws, and he said, "I swear it by my name!"

Silence lay over the isle then, and Yevaud lowered his great head.

When he raised it again and looked, the wizard was gone, and the sail of the boat was a white fleck on the waves eastward, heading towards the fat bejewelled islands of the inner seas. Then in rage the old Dragon of Pendor rose up breaking the tower with the writhing of his body, and beating his wings that spanned the whole width of the ruined town. But his oath held him, and he did not fly, then or ever, to the Archipelago.

BOBO'S STAR

GLENN CHANDLER

WHEN BOBO WOKE up that morning, the star was spinning and burning nicely. He had nursed it from infancy, watched it grow from a cloud of hydrogen gas particles of sand into a hot blue giant. It wasn't really a giant. The star was no bigger, and no more spherical, than a rugby football, but it was his pride and joy, his creation, his very own piece of the universe. He had to wear dark glasses to gaze at it, for the blue-white glare would blind anyone who walked unprepared into the room. Fortunately it was contained by the thick, unsmashable, unmeltable, un-anything-able see-through walls of the anti-gravity chamber, so it couldn't spin off, or set the house on fire, or fall down.

Bobo picked up the instructions for the Star Genesis Kit in his grubby hands and skipped over them impatiently.

Place six pounds of sand in the chamber via the air-lock every day for thirty days, or until your star has formed into a perfect, glowing sphere. Add more hydrogen gas as necessary.

It was the forty-second day, and Bobo's Star – that was the name he had given it – was far from being round. He had one cylinder of hydrogen gas left and a hundredweight of sand. He wondered if he should just tip the lot in and see if it made any difference. Bobo's Star was a hungry object. It condensed matter at a furious rate. Every time Bobo put a sackful of sand through the air-lock, the grains went spinning into it like bath-water down a plughole. The instruction book said that would happen.

Bobo went to the sack with his father's gardening trowel, dragged it over, and began shovelling it in.

"Bobo! Your breakfast's ready. Come down and have it. And wash your hands. And be ready for school!"

Bobo scowled and went on shovelling. His face was dirty and his tie was crooked. When the air-lock was stuffed with sand, he closed the outer door and stuck his thumb on the button which activated the inner one, the one to the vacuum chamber. The hundreds of thousands of tiny orange grains were picked up in a stream by the gravitational pull of Bobo's Star, swung round and round, then swallowed up. Bobo's Star was brighter, but it hadn't changed shape. Bobo was disappointed.

"Bobo, are you dressed?"

"Yes, Mum."

"Then come down this instant. Your breakfast's getting cold. Do you *want* cold bacon and eggs?"

Bobo went downstairs. His father and mother and Uncle Mortimer and little sister Angela were all sitting round the pinewood table attacking grapefruits. Predictably, the bacon and eggs were still sizzling and spluttering in the frying pan.

"Sit down," said his mother. "Eat your grapefruit."

"I don't feel hungry," said Bobo, sullenly.

"You won't grow up into a big boy."

"Why should eating grapefruit make me grow up?" Bobo tossed back at her. "Twenty pounds of sand didn't make a scrap of difference to my star."

"Your star's big enough," stated his father. "Any bigger, and it's going out in the garden."

"I'm starting to wish we'd never bought you that Star Genesis Kit," his mother groused. "For six weeks now we've heard about nothing else. At first we thought it might help you with your physics. But it's become a mania with you, making this star grow. It's not healthy, Bobo, twelve-year-old boys playing at God. They should leave the universe to Him, and not go putting it into the hands of children. That's my opinion."

Uncle Mortimer chortled. His moustaches twitched as he spooned a segment of grapefruit through his chasm of a mouth.

"Leave the boy alone, Cathy," he said. "It's educational."

"It's dangerous," commented Bobo's father.

"It's not dangerous," argued Bobo. "The anti-gravity chamber is built to withstand the heat. It says so in the instruction book."

"What happens if the star falls down?" asked his mother, displaying her not-too-keen grasp of such matters.

"It won't fall down. Look, does the *real* sun fall down?" Bobo waved his grapefruit segment about in the air.

"Yes. At sunset," said little Angela, then, "Ouch!" for Bobo had put his boot into her knee under the table.

"Anti-gravity means it will float there for ever," he explained to his mother.

"Well, it'd better *not* float there for ever," she cautioned him. "I want to do your room out this spring, and I don't want miniature suns and anti-gravity chambers getting in the way. You'll have to shift it."

"Yes, put it in the garden," his father said again.

"Shift it – in the garden – ?" Bobo choked on his grapefruit. "Look, do you know what might happen if I accidentally opened the air-lock into the chamber while the outer door was open?"

"No, and I don't care," said his mother flippantly.

"There would be a WHOOOOOMPH!"

Uncle Mortimer chortled.

"There you are, Cathy."

"Air rushes into a vacuum," Bobo told his mother. "You know what happens when you blow on a fire. The same thing would happen to my star. It would probably flare up so enormously it would come rushing out of the air-lock like a meteor!"

"Don't be silly, Bobo," she dismissed the idea. "Eat your grapefruit. There's vitamin C in it." Then, "Who's ready for bacon and eggs?"

"I am," said Uncle Mortimer, dabbing his whiskers with a monogrammed handkerchief. "By Jove, it's a lad we've got here. He'll make a top scientist one of these days, Cathy. Mark my words."

"Not if he doesn't eat his vitamin C," said his mother.

And that was the end of the matter. Bobo demolished his grapefruit, his bacon, his eggs, his coffee, then went to school. Nobody else at school had a Star Genesis Kit or an antigravity machine. Bobo felt proud. When questioned about it in first-year astrophysics, Bobo got up and with a much-swelled head delivered a narration on how he, Bobo Janson Peters, had created his very own star from the raw ingredients of the universe. It was no mean achievement for a twelve-year-old, even with the aid of a kit. God had taken millions of years to do it, and He didn't have a mother constantly nagging Him to eat His breakfast and keep His room tidy, nor a father continually telling Him to do it in the garden.

When Bobo got home, he went straight to his bedroom, taking the stairs in great jumps. On his door was a sign: BOBO'S STAR – DANGER, WEAR DARK GLASSES AT ALL TIMES. Neither the name nor the injunction were necessary to him. He donned the dark goggles as a course of habit. With them fitted smartly round his head, he stepped into the room. Bobo's Star was still spinning, but it was still rugby-football shaped. Bobo kicked the anti-gravity machine with its unbalanced flywheels and cranks and springs and oscillating weights, but it had no discernable effect on the hot little star inside the chamber. Maybe in order to achieve a perfectly round, healthy, normal, sensible-looking sort of star, he had to feed it with more mass.

He grabbed the trowel and shored up the walls of the air-lock with more sand. The lock was only one foot by two, about the size of a small oven, but it held about twenty pounds at a time. Then he sealed the outer door, opened the inner, and watched the sand spiral in to be sucked up in the blue-white glare. There was no change in the size or the shape. It was infuriating. He hunted round the room for something else that Bobo's Star could eat. Something heavy, like a brick or a piece of metal.

He stole out into the garden, past the vegetable plot where his uncle Mortimer was down on his knees, ferreting about in a bed of lettuce with a spray canister.

"What-ho, young Bobo. What mischief are you up to?" he enquired.

"I'm looking for something heavy. Like a brick," answered Bobo.

"There's plenty of bricks up the top of the garden. Happens your father and I had a few left over when we finished building that wall."

But Bobo didn't stop to listen. There were bricks up the top of the garden. That was good enough. His father didn't get home from work for another two hours, so Bobo could do as he liked with what he liked. Uncle Mortimer was a harmless old fool. He wouldn't interfere.

"I hope you're going to put them back," he chortled, as Bobo disappeared down the path to the house with twenty stacked in a wheelbarrow. Getting them up the stairs past his mother was the tricky part. He had to go through the kitchen where she was rolling pastry. At every journey she twisted her neck and asked him what he had up his jumper, but as her hands were caked in wet dough she didn't bother to investigate herself. Bricks indeed!

Bobo opened the door of the air-lock, and placed the bricks in one after the other. He got them all in, sealed the outer door, activated the inner one. At first it looked as though the bricks weren't going to budge from the lock pad. Then suddenly they shot into a spiralling orbit round the star like a fleet of cumbersome projectiles, their trajectory carrying them nearer and nearer to the stellar surface where they plunged, en masse, into the burning hydrogen soup. Bobo wrapped his hands together and shook them gleefully. Something had to happen to the star. But it didn't. It looked as much like a rugby football as it had done before.

Bobo felt like chucking in the instruction book. What could have gone wrong? Perhaps there were funny-shaped stars in the universe, in the natural universe, perhaps there was nothing technically wrong with his at all, except that it looked wrong.

No, that wasn't good enough. It was only an excuse. Bobo hadn't spent six weeks slaving over a hot star just to end up with an acceptable mutation. If God didn't settle for second best, neither would he. Bobo went to the generator which supplied the power to the anti-gravity chamber, and sent a few shock waves into his private cosmos. They were the sort of shock waves he had sent into the gas at the star's inception. They helped the matter to condense, and ultimately to glow. But nothing happened. The trouble was, the star was generating its own energy now. So it went with stars.

The call for dinner came, but Bobo couldn't eat. He picked at his greens, and ate only half of his lamb chop.

"Our little scientist looks a bit down," observed Uncle Mortimer, chewing on a piece of freshly dug up home-grown marrow.

"I've got a shape problem," said Bobo.

"Eat your greens," said his mother. "They've got vitamins in them."

"My sun won't go round. I mean, it goes round, it rotates. But it won't go spherical. It's like a big hot egg!"

"Maybe you didn't follow the instructions properly," said his father. "It would be just like you, Bobo. Not following the instructions. Always in too much of a hurry, always –"

"Eat those vegetables!" snapped his mother.

Bobo spooned some boiled marrow into his mouth. He hated boiled marrow. It was all stringy and soggy.

"Does your sun have spots?" Angela asked.

"No. Why should it have?"

"All suns have spots. They're called sunspots. If your sun doesn't have spots, then it's not a real sun."

"It *is* a real sun," Bobo took umbrage. "Just climb in beside it and see if you evaporate or not."

"Stop teasing Angela," said his mother.

Bobo sulked.

"Everything that happens in a giant star is happening on a smaller scale up in my bedroom. I started off feeding it with hydrogen. Now it's making helium, soon it will be making carbon, oxygen, nitrogen and ultimately iron for itself."

"Iron? Don't be silly," said his mother.

"It's not silly. That's what stars do. By the fusion of the nuclei of lighter elements to form heavier ones energy is gained through the small loss of mass involved."

Bobo's father choked on a hot sprout. Bobo went on.

"The star makes successively heavier elements as it grows old. Helium is heavier than hydrogen, carbon is heavier than helium, and so on. At each new stage nuclear fusion produces more energy till a reasonable proportion of the star has been turned into iron."

"Remarkable!" said Uncle Mortimer.

"Theoretically," added Bobo, "if you take my star out one day and put it on my bedroom floor, it will weigh so much it'll crash right through into the living room."

"I don't want any of that," his mother warned. "I've just tidied up in there."

"I *was* being theoretical," said Bobo.

"Then be it tidily."

Uncle Mortimer finished his lamb chop. There was custard and treacle pudding to follow. Bobo liked custard and treacle pudding. He shovelled it into his mouth in great steaming gobs.

"You'll burst," said his mother.

"No, I won't."

"Yes, you will. You'll grow fat and burst."

"You will, you will, you will!" shrieked Angela, flouncing up and down in her baby chair, showering everybody with little bits of yellow custard.

"Belt up," said Bobo.

As he licked the last vestiges of treacle from his spoon, it struck him. It was a frightening thought. Bobo's Star grew no larger when he increased its mass. *It only grew heavier.* Theoretically, he could keep feeding it with extraneous matter until it grew so heavy a mere teaspoonful of it would weigh a million tons. For that to happen, of course, he would have to find a million tons of stuff to put through the air-lock. It would be worth a try, thought Bobo.

During the weeks that followed, he shoved as many things through the air-lock as he could lay his hands on. More bricks, bags of sand and gravel, slates and tiles, schoolbooks, old toys, some of his father's tools (they had metal heads and were fairly heavy), an old Imperial typewriter which he found on a rubbish dump, left-overs from dinner, a whole marrow out of the vegetable patch, gardening implements, and a number of pots and pans from the kitchen. The assortment of goods had no visible effect, neither did the volume. Bobo's Star went on spinning and burning even more brightly, like a hungry little animal in a cage constantly begging for more food.

One day, a couple of months later, Bobo had to approach the chamber empty-handed.

"Sorry, Bobo," he said despondently. He no longer felt as though he was talking to himself, for the star had a personality of its own. "I've just run out of objects to give you. And I'm in enough trouble over the things that have been disappearing. You could go on swallowing matter for eternity, burning it up, maybe until I'm dead. And one day Mum's going to make me get rid of you."

That was a point. How was he to get rid of Bobo's Star? A quick consultation of the instruction book led him to the understanding that it should have burnt itself out long ago, ten weeks to be exact. Yet energy was still being released. He could always try filling the air-lock up with water and dousing it that way. But the end of Bobo's Star wasn't something he wanted to think about yet. It might be an old star, and a deformed old star at that, but he looked upon it as a pet, still healthy, still hungry, and still in need of affection. He would nurse it until it died of old age. It was funny to think of stars dying of old age, as though they were alive. Nothing was immortal in the universe. Maybe the universe itself had a grave already dug for it.

Another month passed, and Bobo found more objects, doggedly supplying the star with them. He collected rocks in his father's wheelbarrow, foraged about on the rubbish dump again and brought home over successive journeys nearly a ton of bits and pieces. The star seemed to be losing its brilliance now, but it was still as ravenous as ever. In fact he had never seen it gobble up matter so quickly as it did. About six feet of heavy lead piping shot straight into the spinning, burning ovoid mass as fast as a piece of string might have disappeared up the nozzle of a vacuum cleaner. There was no going into orbit now before being consumed. Bobo's Star just sucked and sucked and sucked.

Over supper that night, Bobo announced, "I think my star's dying. It's getting duller, and it's cooling down."

"Thank goodness," said his mother. "Maybe we'll have

some peace in this house for a change."

"Why do stars die?" asked Angela.

"They use up all their energy," answered Bobo. "In a few days it'll be just a ball of iron."

"You can just get rid of it," said his mother. "I'm not having any balls of iron sitting around the house for people to fall over."

"Put it in the garden," said Bobo's father. "It'll do as a gate stop."

Bobo's father didn't know that there wasn't a gate to stop any more. Uncle Mortimer gave a chuckle, but said nothing. He knew all right. Despising the lot of them for their total inability to grasp the simple physical concepts, Bobo retired upstairs, intending just to go to bed. He put his dark goggles on outside the bedroom door, and walked in. He stopped, shaken by what he saw. Only an hour earlier, Bobo's Star had been the shape of a rugby football, the shape it had been from its inception, the shape Bobo had religiously tried to alter. Now it had drawn out so that it looked like a long, incandescent sausage! There was something ludicrous about the way it continued to spin. Bobo felt like killing it right there and then. It would be like putting it out of its misery. He ran downstairs, filled a pail with water at the sink, and brought it up to the chamber.

"Sorry, Bobo," he said once more. "This is it. We've had great fun together. I've watched you grow from a cloud of gas and a sackful of sand grains. Now you've outlived your usefulness."

With surprising callousness, he placed the pail of water inside the air-lock, and closed the outer door. The moment he opened the inner one, something quite startling happened. The pailful of water just vanished into the elongated star quicker than he could blink his eyes!

Bobo fetched another bucket of water, and tried again. The same thing happened, only this time it happened even faster. Bobo missed the journey across the chamber from the air-lock to the star because it took only a fraction of a second, and he blinked during it. Rather like lightning. You waited ages for it to flash, then blinked at the precise moment it did. Bobo was angry and frustrated. He was fed up with the star, and wanted to see an end of it.

As he pondered gloomily on its fate, the star seemed to elongate even further. It reminded him of the pastry his mother rolled out in the kitchen when she wanted strips to decorate pies – as it grew longer, it grew thinner. Bobo grabbed the instruction book and turned to the last page. As far as he could see, there was no contingency instruction for dealing with the star's end. All it said was that the star *should* burn itself out. *Should*. Instruction manuals were notoriously inadequate. Then he saw the letters in bold red typescript.

WARNING

ON NO ACCOUNT EXCEED THE AMOUNT OF MATTER IN THE CREATION OF YOUR STAR THAT IS RECOMMENDED IN THIS BOOK

That was all. It didn't say what would happen if bricks and garden gates and heavy metal typewriters and lead piping were added. Injunctions were like that. On no account drink. Do not inhale. Do not allow to come in contact with the skin. They never told you what might happen if you disobeyed.

Bobo went to bed, in the hope that the problem might solve itself by morning. It didn't, and Bobo's Star was even thinner and longer, like a long strip of electric spaghetti. It was then that Bobo decided to ask the Spam for his advice. The Spam was the Senior Physics and Astronomy Master, hence the acronym, a tall, willowy man with shrubbery eyebrows and a nose like a hawk. Bobo was top of his class in physics and astronomy, so the Spam was never displeased when Bobo stood up to ask awkward and sometimes difficult questions. It stretched the minds of the rest of the class.

"Sir?" Bobo asked solicitously at school that day. It was the middle of a lesson.

"Yes, Bobo?" the Spam brought his lean, bony hands up to his lapels.

"You know my home-made star, the one I was telling you about?"

"Bobo's Star?" the Spam gave the name full credit.

"Yes, sir. Well – there was something I was wanting to ask about stars in general."

"Go ahead," said the Spam. "Let's all learn something about stars. Listen, class." Then to Bobo, "Well, what is it?"

Bobo looked around. His school mates were all looking bored and disenchanted. Not one of them really believed he had a star at all.

"How many different ways can a star die?" asked Bobo.

The Spam meditated on the question, then replied,

"Three ways, Bobo. Let's see if anyone can tell us what they are. Cuthbertson?"

Cuthbertson woke up. He was ginger-headed with freckles.

"Pardon, sir?"

"Name one way in which a star can die."

"It can blow up into a supernova, sir."

"Correct," said the Spam. He began pacing up and down the aisle between the desks. "A supernova occurs when a really heavy star blows itself to pieces. Some parts of the exploding star may even still be observed streaming out into space from the original site of the explosion, as in the case of the Crab Nebula, visible through quite small telescopes."

He stopped, halfway up the aisle.

"A second way?"

There was a dull silence.

"Come now, what will happen when our own sun finishes its life as a star?"

"Winter, sir?" came a feeble reply.

The Spam frowned.

"Merryman, you tell the class."

Merryman was fat and round, like an apple.

"It becomes a white dwarf, sir," he answered.

"And what is a white dwarf?"

"A cool, dead star, sir."

"Correct. It may well flare up into a nova explosion, engulfing the Earth and probably Mars. But the chances are that our own sun will retire happily in peace and security."

Bobo imagined a sun sitting in its garden, puffing a pipe and bouncing a grandchild on its knee.

"Can anyone tell me a third way?" asked the Spam. "Or rather, tell our young scientist Bobo a third way."

Bobo was jolted back to reality.

"No?"

The class sat silent. The Spam waded down to the blackboard through the sea of ignorance, picked up a piece of chalk, and stabbed the board with it in a dramatic gesture.

"It simply vanishes!" he said with a harsh sibilance.

"Vanishes?" asked Bobo. "How?"

"It becomes so heavy, it collapses in on itself. If we put Merryman in the centre of the floor and get everyone to stand on him, Merryman will be crushed. He will fight back, and try to get up, but the accumulated weight of all the other boys will prevent him from doing so. That is what happens inside a collapsing star."

The class roared with laughter. The boy called Merryman gave a look of bored contempt.

"The star tries to explode," the Spam continued, "but its sheer weight will not allow it to. Instead, it implodes. If we bring every boy in the school and every boy from every other school in the world, and put them all on top of Merryman, Merryman will probably be compressed into something the size of a pea!"

"Good idea," somebody said from the back of the class.

"Sir," asked Bobo, "what happens when it vanishes?"

"It doesn't exactly *vanish*," explained the Spam. "To all intents and purposes it appears to, if we stay far enough away. What happens is that it becomes a black hole, a star so heavy that nothing can escape from it. Not even light!"

A chill went through Bobo.

"Why," said the Spam wisely, "it would be quite impossible to see what was going on in a black hole. The image would be sucked into it! That's why they're called black holes. Things fall into them, and once they've fallen in, you can't see what happens to them. The gravitational pull has become that tremendous."

"Theoretically, sir, a black hole could gobble up the universe," said Cuthbertson.

The Spam nodded his head up and down wildly.

"Quite. Quite," he said.

"And there's nothing you can do to stop it?"

"Nothing," said the Spam, almost gleefully. "If a black hole came into contact with the Earth, our whole planet would disappear into an area perhaps no bigger than a pinhead! Crushed to oblivion!"

The Spam had to sit down. He ran a hand full of knotty knuckles across his forehead. Black holes defied all the laws of science, yet here he was preaching their existence. Nobody quite knew for sure yet.

"Sir," asked Bobo, earnestly again. "What would happen to a star that was shaped like a rugby football?"

"Why don't you shut up?" said Merryman.

"Yes, stop asking stupid questions," said another boy.

But the Spam thought it far from stupid. He was away on a cloud of awesome speculation.

"A rugby football?" he mused out loud. "Interesting, Bobo. Shall we see?"

There were yawns and groans as the Spam picked up the chalk once more. He drew on the board, first a circle, then an oval.

"The spherical star collapses to a single point," he deduced. "Simply because it collapses uniformly about its surface. But our ovoid star – your rugby football, Bobo – would collapse into a thread. A very long thread. A – a thread with no end, getting heavier and heavier until – good grief!"

The Spam turned white as milk.

"If one of those touched the Earth, it would be like being sucked through an extremely narrow letter box, so narrow there would be nothing left of us on the other side."

"And if it was spinning as well, sir?"

The school bell rang. There was a clatter of desk lids and a scuffle of feet.

"I did not dismiss the class!" shouted the Spam.

"Sir – " Bobo spoke up urgently.

"Be quiet, Bobo. We've spoken enough about collapsing stars."

"But sir, this is urgent. You see –"

"Belt up," said Merryman. "We want to get home."

"You might not have a home in a little while," muttered

Bobo despondently.

"Class dismissed," said the Spam.

There was a noisy migration to the door, and out into the yard. Thirty boys trying to squeeze themselves through an area three feet by ten all at once. Bobo thought of Bobo's Star, sucking in, compressing, getting heavier. He felt sick.

"Sir?" he approached the Spam when everyone else had gone.

"What is it now, Bobo?"

"I think – I think – " The words stuck in his throat. "I think I've made a black hole."

"Quite impossible," answered the Spam. "Your star isn't nearly big enough. It would have to be tremendously heavy to collapse so that it became a danger to everything about it."

"But it is heavy, sir. Furthermore – it's collapsing into that thread you spoke about."

"Boyish imagination," the Spam said in a dismissing tone.

"Honestly, sir!"

'You cannot *make* a black hole on the Earth, Bobo. It goes against all the known laws of physics."

"Once upon a time, anti-gravity machines were against all the laws of physics," said Bobo. "Now they're not. I've got a star floating in my bedroom, and it's turning into a monster!"

But the Spam wouldn't listen.

Bobo slung his schoolbag over his shoulder, and walked home, scuffling his feet along the pavement. The sun was shining. He felt very worried indeed. He let himself into the house and without stopping to speak to either his mother or his uncle Mortimer, he walked straight into his bedroom at the top of the stairs. Too late did he remember to put on the dark glasses.

But he didn't need them. Bobo's Star wasn't bright any more. It was so dim he could hardly see it. Now it really was like a thread, spinning round and round in the chamber, like the blade of a propeller.

"Bobo, are you home?"

Bobo didn't answer. He heard his uncle Mortimer coming up the stairs. The whiskered old man peeked round the door, shielding his eyes with his hand.

"It's all right," said Bobo. "It can't blind you any more."

"Thank goodness for that," said his uncle. "Your mother wants a word with you, young Bobo. Seems that half the utensils in the kitchen have gone missing."

That's the least of my worries, thought Bobo.

He followed his uncle downstairs, and faced his angry mother in the kitchen.

"What's happened to my steel saucepan? And the pressure cooker? And the cheese grater, and the heavy frying pan? What have you done with them, Bobo?" she fired at him.

"I used them as fuel in my star," answered Bobo truthfully.

"That blessed star! Well, it's going out, do you hear?"

"Yes, Mum. It's going out," said Bobo.

"And I suppose the garden gate, and your father's tool box went the same way?"

"Yes, Mum."

"And the wall up the top of the garden?"

"Yes, Mum. Brick by brick."

"You are an *evil* child! I've a good mind to put you in with that star."

"You might not have to," said Bobo.

"Now go up to your room. You can stay there without tea or supper as a punishment. It's about time you learnt a little respect for other people's property!"

Bobo turned, and did as he was told. He locked his bedroom door and sat on his bed, waiting for the end of the world. A few hours passed. It got dark outside. The television dinned away downstairs. Bobo read a book, fell asleep, woke up again, read another little bit, began to think perhaps he'd made a mistake. Maybe it was boyish imagination. Maybe Bobo's Star had just burnt itself out, as the instruction book said it would –

He approached the chamber cautiously. He couldn't see the star any more. Instead, there was a long, thin black line spinning round inside. He gulped. There was a knock on the door.

"Who is it?" he asked in a hoarse whisper.

"It's me," said Uncle Mortimer.

Bobo opened the door. It must have gone midnight. Uncle Mortimer was wearing his slippers, winceyette pyjamas, and carrying some toasted teacakes on a plate along with a mug of steaming cocoa.

"I couldn't let you go to sleep without any supper," Uncle Mortimer said compassionately. "I sneaked you this, young Bobo. Your mother doesn't know. Don't you tell her, either."

"I won't," said Bobo. "Thanks."

"Hello – you got rid of your star."

"Don't go too near it, Uncle Mortimer."

"Why ever not?"

"Just don't."

Bobo stayed prudently by the door. His uncle went sniffing round the chamber.

"What happened to all those things you put in?" he asked.

"They've been compressed. Please, uncle, this room is now dangerous."

"Dangerous? Stuff and nonsense, Bobo."

"There's a black hole in there. Believe me."

"A black *what*?"

It was then it happened. The anti-gravity chamber vanished inside itself. The bed was sucked into the thin black line along with the wardrobe, the chest of drawers, the carpet and the bookcase. Uncle Mortimer, the teacakes and the cocoa went with them. The walls began caving in.

Bobo yelled, and flung himself out of the room onto the landing.

"It's happening! It's happening!" he screamed out. "It's the end of the world!"

He was down the stairs, flinging his arms about wildly. The whole upstairs portion of the house disappeared as neatly as a pack of cards drawn up the nozzle of a vacuum cleaner, only the vacuum cleaner along with the nozzle were invisible.

Bobo was out in the street now, and running, his young legs carrying him at a furious pace. He was going to get into dreadful trouble for this. The whole street was being crushed out of existence. His mother and father and little sister Angela and dear old Uncle Mortimer were already part of the pulverized mess. Well, no one had listened to him. It was their fault.

He stopped at the corner of what had once been a row of terraced Victorian houses, and turned back, consoling himself with a single thought. The universe had taken billions of years to create. He, Bobo Janson Peters, was going to destroy it totally, and in a fraction of that time. The black slit would go on spinning, getting longer, cannibalizing everything in its path, beyond the moon, beyond the orbits of the outer planets, to the far-off galaxies and nebulae. The more it swallowed, the more powerful, the more deadly it would become. Whole civilizations would be destroyed by his creation in a single gulp. That made him feel kind of good, kind of important. He'd always wanted to make a contribution to science.

He was standing on that corner, thinking what an impact the headline SCHOOLBOY DESTROYS UNIVERSE would make, when the gravitational pull of the black line sucked him – and the corner – up.

THE YELLOW HANDS

FROM *THE MASTER*

T. H. WHITE

The nightmare in this story is of the kind where you are threatened by some great danger but can't take a step to save yourself. The yellow hands belong to one of the henchmen of 'The Master', an old mad scientist who plans to make himself lord of the whole world. The twins become prisoners inside the rock – kept there, not because physically they can't escape, but because 'The Master' is able to control people's minds . . . It all begins, as the story says, on a beautiful, unnightmarish afternoon.

IT WAS A blistering day in July, and the swell of the sea was like melted lemonade bottles.

The twins lay face down on the hot rock, dressed in nothing but overalls. Nicky was squinting at some stars or pinpoints of light, which the sun threw on the glittering stone three inches from his nose. By letting his eyes go out of focus, these could be made to swim slowly to the left. Judy was fiddling with a broken egg-shell, admiring its thin, curved, fragile smoothness.

In the blue, unwinking sky above them – unwinking but it

made you blink – dozens of sea birds were whirling and circling like snowflakes. As they came between you and the sun, they went brown, then black, and you could see through their wing feathers.

The children's father was sitting with Mr Pierrepoint on the slanting shelf about twenty feet away.

They had their backs turned and were eating sandwiches.

Mr Pierrepoint had a coloured shirt with pictures of Balinese dancing girls painted on it in mauve and electric green. The Duke was dressed in his one-piece rompers, like Sir Winston Churchill's, but his were made of water-proofed cheese-cloth. He had a theory about being porous. He had an oil-skin hat, too, like the man in the advertisement for 'Scott's Emulsion'. Both of them were in good humour.

"My dear sir," the Duke was saying, "do you realize that ours may be the first of human feet to scale this craglet of the wine-dark sea, what?"

"Come again?"

"We are the first people to land here."

"Duke," said Mr Pierrepoint, "it says in the book that St Brendan landed here on his way to discover the States. He was sailing on a mill-stone at the time, and he called the rock by the name of Brandion."

"I know, my dear fellar, I know. But . . ."

"It says . . ."

The twins stopped listening.

Judy put down the egg-shell and said, "All the same, Nicky, it does feel queer."

"What feels queer?"

"Being the First Human Feet."

"I bet we're not, anyway. What about in the last war? All the aircraft went over it – I know that, at any rate. Daddy's information always seems to stop at about 1896."

"Nicky!"

"Well, it does. And how could St Brendan have floated on a mill-stone?"

"It's supposed to be poetical, I suppose. Or religious."

He made one of his sea-faring noises. The cliff on which they were basking was the island of Rockall, which comes in the weather forecasts. It is a granite peak, about seventy feet high, hardly bigger than a large house, and it juts out of the enormous, heaving, lonely Atlantic, some 250 miles north-west from the nearest tip of Ireland.

Once it was part of Atlantis – perhaps – before that continent sank beneath the waves.

Round it, the abyss falls further than the thousand-fathom line. Its fang of stone in the wilderness of water is the single speck which rises above the surface between Britain and America. It is the very home of sun and spray and solitude.

It is true that few people have landed there. For one thing, its loneliness used to make it difficult to find by navigation. For another, it is difficult to land on, being precipitous and often covered by the waves.

Apart from the legendary St Brendan, Rockall has been mentioned a few times in history. Frobisher saw it once, in the spacious days. At that time it was actually wooded, so it must have been higher and larger then. In 1810, a Captain Hall of H.M.S. *Endymion* saw the white droppings of the sea birds on its summit and mistook these for a snowy topsail – so he gave it chase. The landing party which he sent to investigate was cut off by a sudden fog. (Fogs were another of the things which made it difficult to find Rockall. It was not easy in those days to sail 250 miles on a compass bearing and hit a dot which was only seventy feet high.)

Then there was a brigantine called the *Helen,* which was wrecked on an outlying reef in 1824. It is called Helen's Reef even now. But it is strange that a ship should have collided with something no bigger than a ship, in the desert of the Atlantic Ocean. It is as if two fleas walking across a ballroom floor should meet end on.

In 1862, the boatswain of H.M.S. *Porcupine* was sent with a boat's crew to try to scale the place. It was a tossing swell when they came alongside, so no landing was possible. But he managed to grasp a fragment of the island as they rose and fell. He knocked it off with his sounding lead. They brought the bit back to England. It is in the British Museum.

In 1896 – the date which Nicky mentioned – the Royal Irish Academy organized an expedition specially to land there. It made two attempts, at a fortnight's interval, but both attempts were beaten off by the heave of the sea, which was as high as the Himalayas.

Since then, a French research ship has visited and broken off a piece of Rockalite, without being able to land – in 1921 – and a Mr M. T. Bizony swam round the crag on a float lowered from the Fleetwood trawler *Bulby* in 1948. He also managed to chip off some.

As is well known, Great Britain annexed Rockall on 18 September 1955 with a salute of twenty-one guns. This may have been a result of what I am going to tell you.

The reason why Mr Pierrepoint and the Duke had come was so that they could say they had seen such a seldom visited spot, and had managed to land on it. People do these things without more particular causes.

One of the men who tried to climb Everest was asked why he did, and replied, "Because it is there."

Mr Pierrepoint's skipper had found the rock by good navigation and they had scaled it by good luck – using a harpoon gun to throw a rope ashore.

They had been lucky with the weather.

In the offing, the big yacht with its yellow funnel and clipper-like lines – it had a sort of bowsprit – moved slowly round in the sunlight, the skipper worrying about reefs. They could see the Duchess on the sundeck under a red parasol, reading about palmistry, and her Irish setter called Sherry curled up beside her – a brown speck not interested in islands. At the foot of the crag on the west side, the ship's boat lifted and sank like a lift on the breathing bosom of the sea. The disturbed birds circled above them in the fizzling aether. People have claimed to see on or near Rockall: Razor-bills, Puffins, Gannets, Kittiwakes, Guillemots, Fulmars, two kinds of Skuas, Manx Shearwaters and Greater Shearwaters which nest on Inaccessible Island in the South Atlantic. As a matter of fact, it was once believed that the Greater Shearwater nested on Rockall, but of course this is nonsense. No birds nest there.

With an oceanic 'fetch' thousands of miles – all the way from America – the local waves during great gales are at least sixty feet from crest to trough. Breaking surf – the water thrown up on meeting obstructions goes to hundreds of feet. (The lighthouse at Dunnet Head on the Pentland Firth which is more or less in the Rockall area, stands on a cliff three hundred feet high – yet its windows have often been broken by wave-thrown stones.) Those grand storms come four or five times a year. So how could any sensible bird nest on a crag only seventy feet above the surface?

But they do visit the place and they do rest on it.

The Duke had brought a geological hammer with him, determined to out-do the boatswain of the *Porcupine*, and now he set to work.

The noise of his chopping mingled with the strange cries of the gulls.

There was one other living thing on Rockall, and this was Judy's mongrel bitch, whose name was Jokey. They had called her Jokey when she was a puppy, because she really did seem a joke, and a bad one at that. She was such a muddle that all her legs seemed to be of different sizes. She had a long tail, and hair in her eyes, and her coat mostly grew the wrong way, like a hyena's. She looked like a small, untidy, busy charwoman, who had been born in a dustbin. She was about the size of a Skye terrier. Judy loved her more than anything on earth. At the moment, she was yapping.

"Where's Jokey?"

They had to raise their voices because of the gulls.

"She went down there."

"Jokey!"

They whistled and shouted without result, getting only yaps and silences in answer – the silences being for investigation and the yaps for help.

"She must have found something."

"It's probably only a dead bird."

"Jokey!"

"Oh, she's a nuisance," said Judy. "She has probably got herself cliffed or something, and can't get back."

Indeed, the south-east side of Rockall was almost a precipice and they were lying on the edge of it. Or rather, it was two cliffs with a sort of step between them – the top cliff being about twenty feet and the lower one about fifty. There were fairly good foot- and hand-holds – good enough for children anyway, who are lighter in proportion to their energy than adults are.

"Jokey!"

"I suppose I shall have to go and see."

"She's all right."

"But she might fall off."

"Don't *fuss*."

You could almost see what the twins were thinking, as they lay face downwards. Judy was thinking, "Nicky is a man and ought to go, because men do things for women, except cooking." Nicky was thinking, "It is her dog, anyway."

"You would be sorry if she was killed."

"No, I wouldn't."

"Nicky!"

"Why should she be killed?"

"Because it's dangerous."

"Well, go and find her then."

"You ought to go."

"Why ought I?"

"Because."

But it was unanswerable really, for everybody knew that Jokey was Judy's.

There was a resentful silence, except for the saw-mill cries of the Gannets and the clop of the hammer. In the distance, one of the Gannets on coastal patrol spotted a submarine fish, poised for a moment on stalling wing, and fell like a plummet, a thunderbolt, a dive-bomber. It went straight into the sea, plonk, and the little, white fountain of water rose behind it almost lazily into the sparkling air. You could count four slowly, and then there was the dark-looking head on the surface, shaking itself, swallowing the fish. Others of the squadron came to the signal, for it was evidently a shoal, and they peeled off, one after the other, plonk, plonk, plonk. Beautiful dives!

Judy got up complainingly – "a woman's work is never done" – and began to pick her way among the sharp ledges of the rock. Soon she had worked her way round a shoulder of the cliff and vanished.

"Nicky!"

The thin call mixed with the bird noises.

"What?"

"Come here."

"Why?"

"Please come."

"Oh, all right."

He used his grudging voice automatically, but jumped up willingly enough, because as a matter of fact he had wanted to go all the time. Only he had not known that he wanted to.

"What is it?"

"Come and see."

Just below the ledge or step in the cliff face, and clinging rather precariously to a kind of natural shelf or pathway, Judy and Jokey were absorbed in something in front of their noses. Both noses were pointing at it, like the noses of setters, and Jokey's head was on one side, the ears cocked forward.

Nicky made his way down the steepness of granite, putting the shoulder of Rockall between himself and his father. The noise of the hammer died away. Even the cries of birds seemed to fall silent. Now both children were out of sight and out of hearing, even of the yacht.

"What is it?"

"Oh, shut up, Jokey. Don't yap."

The ledge was broad enough to stand on, so she picked the dog up, struggling, and held its mouth shut with her fingers. Jokey was furious.

"It's something in there."

"Where?"

"*Jokey!*"

Kneeling down in the professional way which men have when they are called to mend the plumbing or find out what has gone wrong with the kitchen stove, Nicky examined the rock face where the dog had been sniffing. It was as if the three of them were standing on the keyboard of an upright stone piano. The cliff rose in front of them, where you put the music, and fell behind them to the pedals in the sea.

As a matter of fact, it was more like an enormous pianola. Behind the music rack in these, there is a panel which can be opened, to see the dotted music going round its drums. And straight in front of Nicky, cut in the living rock with the exactness of a cabinet maker, there were the ruled slits or cracks of what looked like a pair of garage doors.

The doors or whatever they were, were not smoothed or planed outside. They were rough and chunky like the rest of the cliff. They had no handles or bolts or visible means of opening them. From a few paces away you could not see the cracks. It was as if a giant with a sharp knife had cut a mathematical square in the side of the island, like cutting a slice of cake without taking the piece out.

"Gee!"

"Jokey says there is something inside."

"It can't be in the crack, Judy. Look, it goes straight up and straight along and down again. And look, it splits in the middle. It must be sort of doors."

"But what's it for?"

"It must be made by men. If it was Nature, it wouldn't be

straight lines."

He ran his fingers along the crack, fascinated by the discovery. Judy, who was about twice as quick on the uptake as Nicky was, began to feel scared.

"Let's go and tell Daddy."

"No, wait a minute. I want to see. Look, if they opened outwards, there would be grooves in the ledge here for them to swing on. They must go inwards. Wait, I want to push."

She stood doubtfully, clutching the wriggling mongrel to her chest, disapproving of the whole affair.

"Let's get Daddy first."

But Nicky was busy shoving at the cliff.

"They must be locked."

"Perhaps they are just natural," she said hopefully, "the result of an earthquake or something? Or a volcano?"

"Ass."

"But Nicky . . ."

At this point one of the doors opened of its own accord, smoothly and ponderously, like the door of a heavy safe.

A pair of yellow hands, with long fingernails like a mandarin's, came from the dark interior − and courteously pushed both children off the cliff.

The Specimen

Tim Stout

CHRISTOPHER WAS READY to give up and go home for the night when he first noticed the strange throbbing.

Since twilight the fifteen-year-old naturalist had been huddling motionless against a tree-stump deep in Noakey Wood, hoping to see the family of badgers emerge from their sett, but after watching for two fruitless hours he was cold and cramped and had grown thoroughly sick of the whole thing. The wretched badgers must have given him the slip. They were probably miles away by now, foraging in the distant meadows beneath the full moon. Well, there was no point in waiting beside an empty burrow. Stiffly he got to his feet. It was while he was making his way to the bush in which he had left his bicycle that the throbbing attracted his attention.

He paused and listened. Just a plane droning by, that was all. And yet the noise wasn't overhead, was it? It seemed to be coming from underneath the ground.

Christopher began to feel uneasy. Not a breath of wind was stirring, yet every tree in the clearing had started to rustle. Birds roosting in the big old oaks were twittering in alarm and quitting their perches. There was certainly something down there. He could sense the vibrations himself, pounding up through the earth.

Whatever was coming, it seemed a good idea to be as far away as possible when it broke surface. He made a dash for his bicycle, but already it was too late to escape. Before he could reach the bush a violent tremor of the earth flung him off his feet.

As the frightened Christopher picked himself out of the bracken he saw the ground tremble as if a giant fist were pummelling it from below. Cracks and fissures appeared around him. He clutched at an oak for support, and felt the sturdy trunk shudder in its roots. Was this an earthquake? Surely not – not in safe, settled England?

The oak creaked, and lurched to one side. There was a colossal eruption of soil followed by a boom like the bellow of a genie set free. A streamlined metal mass the size of a house heaved up out of the ground.

Stones, severed branches and clouds of clay thudded across the clearing. Ten, twenty, thirty feet into the air rose the spinning pillar, thrusting conical shoulders between the trees until its smoking point slowed to a halt high above the woodland floor. Its revolutions ceased, and the clearing settled into a deep hush broken only by the sizzle of damp leaves brushing the hot hull.

Christopher gazed awestruck at the enormous machine. Glittering in the moonlight, it loomed over him like a beckoning steel finger. He stared at the crater of churned clay and his eyes travelled up the dirt-streaked flanks to the flanged tip, which was still smouldering a dull red from the friction of its hurtling passage through the earth. Goodness knows what it was, or how much of it was still below the ground.

Seconds passed. He watched crusts of scorched soil fall from its sides and listened to the slow tick of cooling metal. Nothing happened, and gradually his fear ebbed away. He came out from behind the oak and was tiptoeing forward for a closer look when suddenly a hatchway opened its round black mouth.

From the cylinder's dark interior issued a hollow sigh. Moments later a howling current of air sprang up, snatching at every loose leaf, twig and acorn within the clearing. Christopher tried to scramble for cover in the undergrowth but he too was whisked up like a feather beneath a vacuum cleaner and sucked into the mysterious machine.

Inside, his body landed on something soft. The hail of woodland debris continued, stinging his face and his bare hands. Then the suction was cut off, the howling died away and the hatchway doors rolled together. He was trapped in the belly of the cylinder.

The terrified youngster jumped to his feet. The darkness and silence were absolute. From the popping in his ears and the queasiness in his stomach he realized that the machine was once more on the move, but this time in reverse. Like a modern Jonah swallowed by a steel whale, he was being carried rapidly down into the depths.

He tugged his torch out of his anorak and found that his surroundings consisted of an empty four-walled chamber padded with a spongy, grey material like foam-rubber. It was about the size of a lift, but a lift over which he had not the slightest control.

What in heaven's name was all this? The only explanation he could think of was that it was something to do with the army: perhaps a new kind of missile undergoing secret tests. If there were other people inside, maybe he could arouse their attention. But though he shouted, and banged on the metal doors till his knuckles bled, there was no reply.

Christopher shivered. It was best to face it – he was a prisoner, and there was nothing he could do except wait and see where the cylinder took him.

No sense wasting the torch: there was nothing to look at. He switched it off and sat staring at the sweep hand of his watch as it crawled round the luminous dial. Over a minute had passed when there came a judder, and he heard the faint hiss of air released under pressure. The cylinder had touched bottom – wherever bottom might be.

What would happen now? He waited apprehensively but instead of the hatchway it was the wall opposite which slid back revealing a large window into another part of the machine. Beyond the glass was a second chamber. Christopher gasped. It was occupied – but not by anything human.

In the dim blue glow from the ceiling glinted the coils of a huge serpentine insect. Its black, segmented body was half reared up against the window like a dozen motor tyres that had joined together to go for a climb, and its blunt, scimitar-jawed head was staring him straight in the face. It was motionless and, so far as Christopher could tell, quite dead, but he had no difficulty in imagining what would happen if the hideous thing were capable of squirming out to pin him beneath its orange abdomen and scrabbling claws.

Where in the world could such a monster have come from? Before he was able to puzzle it out, the lift resumed its descent. It was, he realized, moving independently of the now stationary cylinder, sliding down the outside of the glass shaft that seemed to form the core of the machine.

Evidently there were several such show-cases, arranged on top of each other. The next contained what at first glance might have been taken for a deformed dwarf hunched in a tattered grey shawl. As the lift slid slowly past, he studied it closely. Furled wings, gargoyle features, a wicked stiletto of a beak – why, it was a pterodactyl! Christopher stared in disbelief. This was downright impossible: pterodactyls had died out millions of years ago. Yet here it was, not a fossil but the animal's actual body as it must have appeared in life during the Age of Reptiles. What about the monster bug, then? Was that too an extinct creature, perhaps from some epoch even further back in the past when insects had ruled the world? If so it could mean only one thing – aeons before the coming of man, something had searched the surface of the primaeval earth for prehistoric souvenirs.

As the lift came to the next cabinet down, he was startled to find himself face to face with another human being. But could you really call this slouching half-beast a person? Coarse reddish hair swirled over every part of its squat body, and it seemed to be on the point of dropping on all fours and shambling away like an ape. Evolution had certainly moved on from the pterodactyl, but thousands of generations would have to pass before these bristle-browed features saw the dawn of true intellect.

With the occupant of the fourth display-case there could be no such doubts. The armoured knight stood erect in a dramatic fighting stance, his shield slung behind his shoulder and his broadsword gripped in both hands as if he were battling for his life. It was a struggle he must have lost; his blade had snapped off at the hilt and lay at his mailed feet. What, Christopher wondered, had beaten him?

It wasn't very pleasant to think that the suit of armour contained the knight's corpse, but what other explanation was there for the things he'd been seeing? These four figures weren't models or dummies. They could only be the dead bodies of the cylinder's previous victims, dragged down from their worlds as he had been from his, and now preserved uncorrupted behind hermetically sealed glass as exhibits in this eerie museum.

To his surprise the fifth cabinet was empty. From insect to pterodactyl, from pterodactyl to ape-man, from ape-man to mediaeval warrior: was this the extent of the collection? Here the lift halted, and its doors finally opened. His heart beat a rapid tattoo. Perhaps it was now his turn to meet the mysterious collector.

Instead of an exit, the hatchway slid back to disclose a further barrier. Beyond the doors stood two tall close-fitting slabs of polished black stone. The one on his left bore a familiar pattern of coloured lights. Maybe this was the key to the way out.

Recessed into the middle of the slab was a large white globe surrounded by nine concentric grooves spaced outwards like the lanes of a running track. Around the circuit, each following its own course, travelled nine marblesized spheres that twinkled red, green, electric blue and all the shades of a Christmas tree.

Christopher had always been interested in astronomy, and it didn't need the pale ring girdling the sixth sphere to tell him that here was a simple model of the solar system. The central globe obviously stood for the sun and its tiny satellites represented the nine planets, including ringed Saturn, swinging in their orbits around it.

The symbol of the sun re-appeared in the middle of the other door, but here it was encircled by only one empty groove.

What was the purpose of the lights? Surely they weren't just elaborate decorations? He pushed and pulled at the heavy black slabs. Neither of them would budge a millimetre.

Something moved behind him. Turning, he saw that the glass panel between the lift and the display-case had slid open. The cabinet was no longer empty. To his horror, hundreds of finely-pointed metal rods were now protruding from the far wall. Like spikes in some ancient engine of torture, they crept stealthily towards him. So this was how the knight had died, shattering his sword against a phalanx of lances so tiny they must have pierced his armour invisibly. Christopher forced himself not to panic. Unless he kept cool and used his head he too would be impaled and drawn back into the display-case to become the gallery's latest exhibit. He looked back at the doors and racked his brains for a solution to the riddle of the lights.

And then it came to him. They were nothing but a simple intelligence test. The slab on the left posed the question – did he know what the solar system was? The slab on the right provided him with a blank answer-sheet. Its empty groove was surely meant to accept one of the nine planets, but which was he supposed to choose? A random selection made no kind of sense. What if he transferred the Earth symbol? Assuming he picked the right one, wouldn't that prove to whatever forces controlled this place that at least he knew enough about the universe to recognize his own world's position within it? Perhaps this would produce the 'open sesame' he needed.

Facing the black slabs, he counted outwards from the sun. First, amber Mercury. Then shining Venus. Earth came third. Breaking the slight magnetic tug he plucked the little blue lamp from its orbit and inserted it in the empty groove. At once the miniature planet began circling its new sun, but still the doors remained closed.

Something caught at his anorak. The pointed rods were now almost upon him. Another five seconds, and he would be pinned like a captured butterfly.

As he beat his fists frantically against the barrier there came a sigh like a giant awakening. The ponderous slabs rolled slowly back. Sobbing with relief he squeezed between them – and found himself falling through space.

The concealed chute delivered him shaken but unharmed to the edge of what seemed at first to be a subterranean lake. Then he realized that what he had taken for the sheen of water was a wide metal floor gleaming in the blue glow now creeping across the domed ceiling of a large, circular chamber. The air here was cold and still as if the room itself were dead, but the feeling came to him that at last he was in the presence of the power that directed the movements of the cylinder.

As the light grew stronger he saw that the middle of the floor sloped down into a round hollow shaped like a sunken bath. It was covered by a sheet of translucent green ice, now melting beneath the glowing ceiling to form a drifting phosphorescent haze.

At the bottom of the hollow, a long form stirred. Christopher froze with excitement. There was somebody down there, lying underneath the thawing ice.

Abruptly, the light faded. The shape rose to greet him.

Christopher retreated warily. "Who are you?" he whispered.

There was no spoken reply. Instead, from the shadows, there came a soft, owl-like hoot.

He switched on his torch and, as its beam played over the tall, thin figure hobbling towards him, he cried aloud in fear.

For a brief instant two enormous black eyes stared at him out of a white, gelatinous face. Then the spindly form winced and hid its pointed, high-cornered head in its hands as though the sudden light had injured it.

The terrified youngster cowered back. How could this naked, pale-skinned creature be shaped like a man, when everything else about it looked like those pale, glistening grubs you found under damp stones?

It came groping forward and seized his shoulder with chill, bluish-white fingers. Through the sleeve of his anorak he felt the pulpy pressure of their grip as they slithered down his arm, wrenched the torch from his grasp and crushed it like a paper cup.

He turned to run. Where to, he had no idea. Then he slipped on the fragments of the fallen torch and struck his head on the floor, losing consciousness.

When he awoke he was sprawled at the side of the room with his head cradled on his folded anorak. The creature seemed to have tried to make him comfortable. Around him, the cylinder was coming to life. He could hear the hum of concealed machinery and feel its vibrations through the floor.

Now the ceiling light had been turned up again, and in the dim blue glow he saw that the chamber's eerie occupant was studying a range of dials and flickering instruments set in its walls. It saw that he had regained consciousness and came towards him, slowly and calmly, as he himself would have approached a frightened animal. Since escape was out of the question he had to hope that it meant him no harm.

From a cleft between its intelligent black eyes issued a series of the low, tremulous hoots he had heard earlier. To Christopher's astonishment, they turned into thoughts inside his head. At first all he picked up was a warm, reassuring mental glow. Then the words began to come through.

"Don't worry," the creature was saying. "You're perfectly safe."

The idea of conversation with this unearthly spectre was so incredible that Christopher hardly knew how to react. "Why can I understand you?" he asked.

The hoots came again, and once more the figure seemed to speak to him. "Mind," it said, "is the true speech of the universe."

"The universe?"

"Certainly. What else but mind can bridge the gulf between your world and mine?"

A man from another world? From space? Christopher tried, but after everything that had happened to him since the cylinder had engulfed him he just couldn't find the right emotion to deal with such a concept. He knew he ought to say something clever or important, something for the history books, but the best he could do was to ask, "Where are you from?"

"I do not know what your people call it. I know it as —" The figure uttered a word that sounded like "Lupercos". "My own name is Kharool."

Christopher's mind was a whirlpool of questions. He seized one at random. "Why have you come to Earth?"

"My race longed to probe the secrets of the universe and to discover whether intelligent life existed elsewhere than on our own world. Our finest minds devised a projectile to cross the wastes of space and imbed itself deep within the fabric of another globe – a trap that would lie far underground, unseen and unsuspected, but which would from time to time rise to the surface and gather samples of whatever was to be found there.

"The pilot was given the means to place himself in suspended animation after landing. He was to wait, inert within the projectile, for whatever time might pass. The life-giving radiance that would revive him could only be brought into play by the operation of a mechanism designed to tax the mentality of whatever life-forms were obtained.

"I was that pilot. Your world, our nearest neighbour in space, was our target. And you are the first specimen of sufficient intelligence to rouse me from my rest."

Christopher felt terribly afraid. For untold centuries Kharool had been lying in the Earth, waiting for his rocketship trap to catch him something worth waking up to interview. He was hardly likely to let him go after a five-minute chat.

"What are you going to do with me?" he asked, knowing the answer before he spoke.

"Haven't you understood?" Kharool gazed at him with black, unfathomable eyes. "You will return with me to Lupercos."

"But my home is here, on Earth!" He felt like a prize carp, pleading with the angler to throw him back.

"Surely your own men of science search for life on other worlds?"

Christopher thought of the Viking probe to Mars. "Yes, but

82

only to collect soil samples."

The visitor from space looked round at the interior of his cylinder. "Do you think they would be content to grub about in the soil if they possessed a piece of equipment like this?"

His cold, pallid hand gave Christopher's arm an almost paternal squeeze. "Don't worry. We'll look after you. Lupercos is a beautiful place. Come and see for yourself."

From a wall locker he produced a dozen or so discs of transparent metal, printed with colour views. Christopher stared at the snapshots from space. Lupercos, it seemed, was a world of darkness and shadows. There were craters, great canyons and rivers of what looked like frozen yellow gas, stretching in sombre solitude beneath a louring green sky.

It was a gloomy looking place, he thought, but Kharool obviously didn't think so. His cadaverous white features were softened with longing for his own world. The boy felt a pang of pity for this creeping shadow-dweller who had never known the pleasure of a clear sky or a sunny day.

The last picture showed a strange pyramidal structure of jagged grey rock. Dotted all over it were clumps of shimmering red stones.

Kharool pointed at it proudly. "This is my home. I raised those tyrelligon crystals myself, by chemical grafting."

Producing a piece of red stone the size of a fountain pen he rubbed it with one finger. At once the crystal gave off a bright glow that shone in his black eyes like a burning coal. "I brought this with me to your world, as a reminder of my own."

He hesitated, then gave it to Christopher. "Accept it as a gift."

The sound of the cylinder's engines had now risen to a pulsing throb. Kharool opened a door in the wall of the chamber. "Excuse me, please. The projectile's motor is operated automatically but there are some adjustments to make before we take off."

As soon as the alien had disappeared Christopher ran to the chute down which he had fallen into the chamber but, as he had feared, it was far too steep to climb. He slumped back against the wall. Space-napped – taken away from his home, his parents and everything he knew to spend the rest of his life on another world. It was just too terrible to think of.

Where *was* Lupercos, anyway? Kharool had said that Earth was its immediate neighbour. That narrowed the choice to two planets: Mars and Venus. The green sky argued against dusty red Mars but Venus, with its surface temperature of eight hundred degrees, seemed just as unlikely.

Then another possibility occurred to him. If he was right, it changed everything. Perhaps it even offered a faint hope of escape.

When Kharool returned he found Christopher still studying the pictures of Lupercos. He laid a hand on his prisoner's shoulder. "Come, we must get ready. I have prepared a cubicle in which you will be able to pass the flight in comfort."

Christopher turned to him, "Let me see outside just once more."

"I'm sorry. We don't have the time."

As the young boy's eyes filled with tears, Kharool reached out to touch them. "What are these?"

Christopher twisted away, and instead of his face the groping white hand caught his hair. Out fell an acorn. It must have been lodged there when he was sucked into the cylinder.

Kharool picked it up for a closer look, but in his clumsiness squashed it into a sticky green mess.

Suddenly Christopher had an idea. With a cry of feigned despair he retrieved the acorn's remains and placed it beside Kharool's red crystal.

"You knew when you were going to leave your world. You even had time to bring a souvenir. But I'll never see Earth again, and now you've destroyed all I had to remind me of it. Please let me go outside for the last time!"

The man from space paused. Christopher held his breath. So much depended on whether he had read his captor's character right. Could he make Kharool feel sympathy for him?

The alien didn't reply for a moment. Then his thoughts spoke in Christopher's mind. "As you wish. But it will not be for long."

A few minutes later they were standing side by side at the threshold of the cylinder. Christopher almost fainted with pleasure at the pungent odour of the wet wood. Only now, as he sucked in the fresh night's air, did he realize how stuffy it had been in the cylinder's metallic depths.

The huge machine had surfaced in exactly the same spot.

He peered around for what he had been hoping to see but there were too many trees in the way. Somehow he would have to persuade Kharool to venture outside. If he failed, then this would be the last he would ever see of his own planet.

He turned to the tall white figure beside him. "Surely you don't want to go home without a look around?"

Kharool hesitated. Christopher sensed that outside his own metal surroundings he felt uneasy, but the dark wood seemed to intrigue him. Perhaps they had forests like this on Lupercos.

"Very well," he finally agreed, and the two stepped out of the cylinder. Kharool's strong fingers kept firm hold of his priceless scientific specimen. He was peering with interest at the trees, stroking their bark with his free hand, when Christopher suddenly caught sight of what he had been searching for so desperately.

It was literally now or never. He tugged at Kharool's arm. "Look!"

"Where?" The man from space turned to follow his pointing finger – then shrieked in agony as the full moon stabbed at his sensitive eyes.

He threw up both his hands to cover his face, just as he had done to protect himself from Christopher's torch. Immediately the youngster pulled free, and rushed across the crater of churned clay until he was out of reach.

Kharool made no move to pursue him. Hands clasped to his eyes, he doubled up in pain. "What is it?" he moaned.

"It's the moon!" Christopher shouted. "Don't you recognize it? It's our nearest neighbour in space – your own world!"

"Impossible!" The alien clawed at his face in pain and misery. "Lupercos is a world of green skies, with its own atmosphere."

Christopher knew he was safe. After an eternity underground Kharool's sensitive eyes were too feeble to recover from the shock of gazing full at the moon's bright, airless disc. "The atmosphere leaked away long ago," he called across the clearing.

"No!"

"Astronauts from Earth have been up there. We know what it's like. It's just a lump of dead rock."

"No! It is a living world. My people are waiting for me to return."

"Not any more. You came to Earth millions of years too soon. While you were hiding in the ground hoping for intelligent life to develop here, it was dying back on your own world."

He ran to his bicycle, then looked back and saw Kharool stumbling towards the hatchway of the cylinder. A rush of pity swept over him.

"Kharool!" he shouted.

The weird, pointed head turned. Even at this distance Christopher could see that the dark eyes were now blind, as dead as the moon itself. He felt a stab of guilt.

"Kharool," he called again. "I'm sorry!"

Then, grabbing his bicycle from the bush, he ran as fast as he could from the clearing.

It took him a couple of minutes to get clear of Noakey Wood. As he rode out onto the moonlit country road, he heard a mighty rumble swell out of the trees behind him.

A huge silver shape burst up out of the wood on a pillar of fire, then thrust high into the clear night sky.

Christopher felt in his pocket for the crystal Kharool had given him. He rubbed it against his sleeve and watched the crystal flare. Then it faded as the cylinder shrank to a pinpoint of light between the hills and the moon.

He waited until it had vanished, then turned his handlebars towards the long road home.

OF POLYMUF STOCK

JOHN CHRISTOPHER

I WAS BORN true man but of polymuf stock. Until I was nine years old I knew nothing of this. I was the son, it seemed, of Andrew Harding, the chief of the Captains in the Prince's council. The Hardings were one of the oldest and noblest families in the city. I had an elder brother, Gregory, and two elder sisters. I lived in the great Harding house which looked at the Palace from across the square, and though smaller was not much less magnificent. I had a polymuf nurse and polymuf servants in plenty to do my bidding.

One day I found myself alone in a poor part of the city near the East Gate. I had been with a friend but we had quarrelled and separated. The quarrel was over nothing and probably came from disappointment. I had a new kite and we had meant to fly it from the grazing meadows but the day was hot and still and it would have been a waste of time to try. I suppose the sultry heat, to which we were little accustomed, tried our tempers also.

It was probably the heat which made me think of going outside the city into the country. I had never done this on my own but was in a mood to explore. The East Gate was the nearest and I made for that, but lost my way in the warren of mean streets and alleys that surrounded it. The houses looked pinched and crowded and badly in need of repair, and there were smells that made me wrinkle my nose. A dead cat which I saw in a gutter must have been there close on a week.

In one crumbling rotting street I found three boys of about my own age following me. Their tunics were of cheap cloth and could have done with mending, and both they and their clothes would have been better for washing. They jeered at me and I ignored them; then came past and planted themselves in my path. One demanded my name and I told him: Isak Harding. It made matters worse because they were Blainites.

The Hardings and the Blaines had been rivals for generations. This was for the most part hidden under a show of politeness but at a lower level, among the followers of each family, the feud was more open and more bitter. The three young Blainites were delighted, I suppose, to find a Harding in their territory and at their mercy. They would scarcely have dared touch me, since I was noble, but taunts leave no marks. They made plenty of these and in the end it was I who turned to violence. I picked on the chief of my tormentors, who also happened to be the biggest, and launched myself at him.

Had things been equal I would have been no match for him because he was stronger as well as taller and plainly used to rough fighting. But he was held back by the realization of my rank – the son of a Captain – and probably by the thought that even if he beat me retribution was likely to follow. I had no such scruples and bore him to the ground. I had him pinned and was rubbing his face in the dirt when we were pulled apart and lifted to our feet. A crowd of older people had collected.

Questions were asked and my name required again. When I gave it one man said, "Isak! That's the one who . . ."

He dropped his voice to a whisper which I could not catch. I heard other whispers and saw glances exchanged. I saw smiles and sniggers. It meant nothing at the time except that they were Blainites. I noticed with satisfaction that my recent opponent was crying and turned from them. I had gone several paces when I heard a voice cry, "Polymuf! The Harding polymuf brat."

That meant nothing either. It was nonsense. I knew I had no malformation of the body. I walked on, heading back towards the city's centre. Boys followed me, chanting, "Polymuf! Polymuf!"

It was some new stupidity the Blainites had thought of to insult their betters; no more than that. I came into Bird Street and there were troopers comparing notes about the finches that hung in cages outside the shops, and the boys fell back and left me.

I forgot about it the same day, or thought I did. Then a month later I heard the jeer repeated in the street. After that I noticed other things: curious looks, conversations broken off when I came within earshot. I still did not believe they could signify anything real or important, or I would not have spoken of it to David Greene, the one with whom I had quarrelled in the summer.

He knew nothing either but he asked, and was told, and told me.

Every child that was born had to be taken to the Seer in the Seance Hall, to be scrutinized for defects of the body. Those that had none were classed as true men, and the short-legged ones as dwarfs. The others, even where the deviation was no more than an extra finger or toe, or one less than was normal, were polymufs, whose destiny was to serve true men, who had no rights and could own no land or property.

If a child was born dwarf or polymuf from human stock it was taken from its mother and given to a dwarf or polymuf foster-mother to rear. The reverse was true also. And this, David said, had happened in my case. I had been brought to the Seance Hall by polymuf parents, judged true man by the Seer, and given to the Hardings.

I listened with shock and horror. It was one thing to feel unease, to suspect vaguely that there was something which needed explaining; quite another to face such as this. I saw David's eyes watching me. He was not smiling but I read the smile behind them, and more: pity and contempt. I said, "It is a lie!"

He shrugged. "Perhaps. It is what they say."

I felt myself shivering and forced my limbs to stillness; but they would not be still. So I made an excuse to leave him and ran back to the house. It was a cold grey morning, threatening rain. The doorman rose from his stool to salute me, his right shoulder lifting from his twisted back.

My nurse Betty was seeing to my room. The housemaids

had already cleaned it but she was never satisfied with their work and must always do a final tidying and setting to rights. I had meant to put the question to her – was this story true? – as soon as I found her, because as long as I could remember I had taken questions and troubles to her for answering and soothing.

But she looked at me from her single eye, just a little to the right of the nose bridge, and I could not do it. Knowing her from an infant I had grown used to her appearance: I recognized the deformity but it had meant nothing. Suddenly it meant a great deal, and I felt revulsion and a nausea that made my stomach heave. I turned quickly and ran. She called after me but I paid no heed.

I ran out of the house and across the courtyard behind. I was heading for the stables, another familiar refuge on bad days and one which unlike Betty had no connection with my present shame. I was weeping as I ran. My eyes blinded with tears, I could scarcely see where I was going. As I reached the stables a man came out and I ran into him. I was checked and held and my father's voice said, "What haste, boy?"

I looked up and could not speak. He said, "And tears? A Harding does not cry, when he is nine years old."

I said, gasping, "A Harding, sir? Or a polymuf's brat?"

He stared at me, his face closed and seeming hard. I thought he would strike me and almost welcomed the thought. But after a moment he said, "We have talking to do, Isak. Come with me."

He was not a tall man and was sparely built. His face, too,

was thin, with keen blue eyes and a well trimmed beard, turning white. It had never occurred to me before to look for resemblance to my own dark heavy features in him, but I did so now, then turned my head away.

We sat in his business room, with the parchment rent rolls hanging on their sticks on the wall and logs crackling brightly and noisily in the hearth. He was a man who felt the cold and sought warmth where he could. He sat in his big chair, covered with the chestnut hide of a favourite horse that had been killed under him in battle, and I on a leather stool before him. He said, "The tears have stopped. Good. Now tell me what you have heard."

I would have broken down again in the telling but his cold eyes forbade it. When I had finished, I said, "Is it true, sir?"

He nodded and said, "As far as it goes."

I started to sob and he put a steadying hand on my shoulder.

"A Harding does not cry."

"But I am none!"

"You are."

"I am not your son."

"No," he said, "but of my line and blood. You are my grandson, Isak."

I stared, uncomprehending. He said, "My first-born child was a girl. The Seer named her polymuf and she was taken from us. It is the law, and the Spirits command it. My wife grieved and died within two winters. Later I married again and my children were whole and human. These are your sisters

94

and your brother."

He paused and I waited. He went on, "Then the Seer came to me. A polymuf woman had given birth to a boy who was true man and must be given to true men for rearing. The woman was my daughter. My wife and I took you to rear as our own. You are my own, a Harding."

"My mother . . ."

"Has doubtless had other children."

"Who is she? Where does she live?"

He shook his head. "We do not know."

"But . . ."

"It is the law, Isak. The Seer knows these things but no other may. I was not told to whom she was given, nor she that you were given back to me. The Seer told me whose was your ancestry because it seemed fitting. And I . . ." He paused again. "I thanked him, and thanked the Spirits, and made an offering which he called generous. But it was a poor return for what they had given me."

"And my father?"

"Who knows?"

Who knew, indeed? I thought of the polymuf men I had passed unthinkingly in the streets, or in the house itself, with limbs too many or too few, with all the diversity of crookedness and ugliness which the evil Spirits were said to wreak on the unborn child. I thought of Grog, who used four arms to sweep the streets, and Petey who apart from a hunched back had a double row of teeth in his jaw, and showed them when he laughed gapingly for the troopers who bought him ale. Any one of them might have been my father.

"And it does not matter," my grandfather said. I stared at him, hot-eyed. "You are a Harding. Those who have dared to mock you will regret it."

I do not know what word went out nor what punishments were inflicted, but there were no more cries of "Polymuf" after me in the street. The Hardings, as I have said, were a powerful family, my grandfather the most respected of the Prince's companions. He told me to forget what I had learned and made sure that none reminded me of it.

But there was no need of reminder. What I had learned sank deep into my mind and lay there with the cold weight of iron. Polymufs, whom I had previously taken for granted, became monstrous to me. Even Betty, whom I had loved, turned repellent. I shivered away from her touch and the gaze of her single eye.

It was customary for a boy of noble family to leave home at eleven for his spell of life in barracks. I begged to go when I was ten, and it was granted. When I returned it was with a different status and to a different room from the one that had been my nursery. I no longer required a nurse and Betty retired to the servants' quarters. I saw her from time to time and smiled and nodded but did not stay to talk with her. I believe she thought me changed and cruel, but I could do nothing else.

I returned from barracks with high praise from my Drill Sergeant. Although younger than the others, he said, I showed more promise; he had rarely known a boy so keen to excel.

The fact was that in drilling, working, learning the arts and crafts of soldiering, I could forget what I was in the ambition for what I might be. And I loved the barracks, a place of true men where no polymuf was permitted to enter. I grew drunk with the smell of horses and leather, the clash of swords and the sharp jingle of harness. The hardships of life I accepted exultantly: these were trials for true men.

Among the other boys, too, I was respected. On my first day I fought a bigger boy and beat him. He had made a remark to which I took offence – not concerning my ancestry but the cut of my tunic. He tried to pass it off but I would not let him. I beat two others also and after that they fought shy of provoking me.

I had no friend and wanted none. They talked about me, I guessed, behind my back – maybe called me "Polymuf" when I was out of hearing. But none would hold his gaze against mine, and they watched their words when they spoke to me. I did not mind if they liked or disliked me. It was enough that they dropped their eyes before mine, and guarded their tongues.

So the later years of my childhood passed, during a time in which great events happened in the city. Prince Stephen was deposed by the Captains and replaced by Robert Perry. My grandfather should have been elected but the Blaines blocked it, preferring a man they thought more easily controlled and of no lineage. Intrigue and murder followed and within two years we had a new Prince, Robert's son, Peter, and his younger son Luke was taken into exile by the Seer, to live with the High Seers in Sanctuary. Later Luke returned and fought and killed his brother and became Prince in his place, our third within three years. And next spring, being thirteen, I was named as one of the Young Captains to fight in the Contest.

The Contest which was held every year was a tournament in which four sons of Captains led teams of boys against one other, each having four followers. Teams were eliminated in turn as their Captains were unhorsed until one was left as victor. The swords used were only of wood and blunt, but they could hurt. It was no sport for weaklings.

I was determined to win the Contest and the jewelled sword which was the Young Captain's prize, and spared no effort. The first concern was to find the best men for my team. My reputation helped because I myself was known as the best swordsman and one of the two best horsemen of my year; and those who fought with the winning Captain would receive gold. But I made sure of the ones I wanted by promising to double the sum, relying on my grandfather's pride in my achievement to make good the promise. Then I drilled them, day after day, relentlessly; beyond the bounds of what was seemly but I kept them to it.

Lastly I made alliances. It often happened that two Young Captains would agree to fight first against a third and eliminate him. Robin Becket, my chief rival, offered me such an arrangement. I accepted but found excuse not to seal it with a handshake. Then I went to Peter Gray, whose team was reckoned third in strength and with him made a bargain for the first round, and sealed it.

I had left no room for things to go wrong, and nothing did. Robin was confused and shaken when Peter and I rode together against him, and he put up little opposition. It took not much more than five minutes' fighting to bring his fall, and the clang of the bell for the first interval. When the fight resumed I set my men at Peter and here again I had the advantage of surprise: our agreement had been for the first round only but he had assumed we would stay allied to eliminate Ranald, whose team was the weakest of the four. Ranald, seeing the change, joined with us – to survive into the last round was more honour than he could have hoped for.

Peter fought hard and three of Ranald's men were down before my sword caught him under the ribs and lifted him out of his saddle. But all my four were mounted still. We waited calmly for the last bell, drove Ranald into a corner and overthrew him.

It was the shortest Contest any could remember, and the first for many years in which a team had come through to victory without losing a man. I led my pony to the Prince's pavilion with cheers from the mob seeming to echo against the sky and the bushy top of Catherine's Hill. No one now was shouting "Polymuf". Luke, our Prince, only a few years older than myself, proffered me the hilt of the jewelled sword which I had won. He said, "You fight well, Isak."

"Thank you, sire."

"And hard. The surgeon says that Peter has a rib stove in from that last thrust of yours."

"Must one not fight hard in battle, sire?"

"In battle, yes."

He looked as though he would say more but did not. I raised the jewelled sword to salute him, and the crowd howled even louder.

My victory was not popular among those of my age and class. Their resentment showed in their faces and there were mutterings. It was whispered that Robin, feeling himself to have been cheated, would challenge me to a duel, on foot with wooden swords, man to man. When I heard that, I took the trouble to seek him out. He sat with friends on the steps of the Buttercross. I stood and looked at him, but he said nothing.

I knew I was a match for any one of them in any kind of fight they chose, and it did not trouble me to be disliked. I was certain at least that they would neither despise nor pity me. I had grown used to my own company and was satisfied with it. I spent much time in the barracks still, schooling myself to be a warrior. Sometimes at night I stood on the city's walls and looked out down the Itchen valley, and thought of the future.

It was through arms that a man achieved success in life, but it was not military glory that provided the seal on success. It was wealth which did that. My grandfather had been a warrior, as all men of rank must be, but neither skill nor courage had given him the position he held in the city and the council of the Prince. It stemmed from the gold which flowed into the city from his farms.

So to triumph as a warrior was not an end but a means. In war one gained booty, and the better one fought for one's Prince the more one got. I vowed I would earn and get a lion's share, and the gold I gained I would not waste. Gregory was my father's true son and therefore his heir, but the day would come when I outranked him.

Glory meant wealth and wealth meant power. Men had believed once that no commoner could ever rise to the rank of Prince, but Luke's father, Robert Perry, had given the lie to that. They would say it was unthinkable that someone born of polymuf stock could reign. But it was not unthinkable, for I thought it.

I toughened body and mind for the task I had set myself. In the streets of the city I walked alone and others gave me room. I scarcely noticed them. The ones I did see, always with a shiver of revulsion and disgust, were the polymufs. That one, the giant nearly eight feet tall – was he my father? And the stooping woman, with a cloth pulled across to hide her face – was she my mother?

When we rode out on the campaign I went with the army. As a scout only, but it made a start. We rode against Romsey, with whose Prince our own had a score to settle.

His name was James and he too was young, but wily. He brought his army out of the city but on the far side of the river on which it stood. He edged southwards along the valley and our army followed on the opposite bank. It was a progress in fits and starts, with each side looking for an advantage but finding none sure enough. Two days passed in this way. It was something that the weather held fair; cloudy but warm and dry.

On the second night I was one of the scouts on the

extreme southern flank. I was given a post on high ground some distance from the river, from which, at dawn next day, I could be expected to see the Romsey outriders and report any change in their disposition. I took my place as evening faded into night. The sky, I noticed, had almost emptied of cloud and the air was very calm. In the valley white mist rose from the river's tumbling surface and spread out, still rising, over its banks.

It reached me in the small hours of the night, a thin cold miasma that clutched at throat and eyes. I could see nothing for the dark, but I could feel it. The only thing to do was wait and hope it would clear with the rising of the sun.

It was a long night. The mist itself was black and unchanging, and it seemed to have stifled the strange small sounds of the night: the owl's cry, the swish of grass or crackle of thicket at an animal's passing. There were only long minutes and longer hours. At last, slowly, very slowly, the blackness turned to grey and the grey lightened to pearl. No more than that. I could make out a brightness in the east which told me the sun was up but if I stretched my hand out before me, my fingers turned shadowy and tenuous. I could scarcely see my feet.

I had been given no orders to cover this case. I could stay where I was until the mist lifted, or try to make my way back to the army. I decided on the latter, not through loneliness or even hunger – I had finished my hard rations during the night – but because it seemed the better course. I could do no good here and the mist, for all I knew, might last all day.

I could not see my way, and the first thing a scout learns is not to call for help except in extremity. The answer, I thought, was to get down to the river. If I turned right on reaching it I should eventually make contact with the others. I might, with the mist as thick as it was, find myself in the water first but that did not worry me. At any rate, I could not miss it.

Or so I thought: it was a simple matter of heading down the slope till I reached the river. But the slope, as I learned later, was not continually downwards; there was a ridge that intervened and there, unable to see anything but the ground a foot or two ahead and groping painfully forward, I must have turned south instead of west.

Time was meaningless as distance but at last I realized that I was lost. I tried to work out where I might be and to correct my course but soon realized the futility of it. I was not just lost, but hopelessly so.

I knew now I must stay where I was, because any move I made was only likely to make matters worse. I must wait until I could see my way. And the mist did seem to be thinning and growing lighter. I saw the brighter pearl in the east tinged with fitful yellow and at last with gold. Then a pale disc, shown and lost again. And the sun and with it the mist broken and lifting all round. I peered about me, trying to get my bearings.

It was not easy. I was in rough country, with coarse rabbit-cropped grass and patches of scrub. In most directions the ground rose, and I could see nothing of the river. But close by there was a mound, grassed and thorned in places, which offered a vantage point.

As I climbed it I realized, from the bricks and the looseness underfoot, that this was a ruin from ancient days, before the Disaster. Such places were thought by simple people to be the haunt of evil Spirits, bound there by the Disaster into which they had led mankind, and therefore shunned. These were not the sort of fears that had ever troubled me and I had no apprehension. Even when the slope collapsed under my feet and I found myself falling, I did not think of Spirits. The rubble was unsafe, that was all: I cursed my foolishness in not taking more care.

And after that I was only concerned with trying to break my fall and with fending off loose bricks that flew around me. I dropped a long way and landed on one knee, so painfully that I thought I had broken my leg. The dust and rubble settled about me while I writhed in pain. After a time I could rub it and feel that there was no fracture. It hurt but I could move, even sit up. There was room to do that; I was not pinned down as I so easily might have been. High up a jagged hole framed the sky. Very little light came from it – I could see almost nothing of my surroundings. I felt in my pack, which had fortunately not been dragged from me in the fall. I found my tinder-box and a stub of candle. I lit it and could see again.

I was in a room whose ceiling I had crashed through at one corner. Rubble that had come with me lay scattered on the floor but only in this spot. The rest of the room was untouched. And furnished. I saw chairs, a long table, a sideboard against the far wall. Table and sideboard were piled with objects that were covered with dust and cobwebs, so that one could not make out the individual shapes but only a jumbled mound.

The table was nearer. I climbed painfully to my feet and approached it. One of the first things I recognized, at the table's edge, was a candle. I lit it from my own; it flickered then burnt more brightly. A drop of melted wax made a hole in the coating of spiders' webs surrounding its holder. The candlestick was of metal. I rubbed the dust away and saw a soft yellow gleam. The metal was gold.

I looked at the other objects on the table. There were pots and plates, more candlesticks, salvers, jugs, vases. Some were gold and the rest, though badly tarnished, were plainly silver. I moved to the sideboard and found other treasures. Lidded pots, with handles and spouts to pour from, silver dishes whose sides were worked in a delicate pattern of leaves and fruit, the fruit something like gooseberries but weirdly clustered together, a heavy intricate chain of gold . . . The sideboard had cupboards under it. The door of one sprang open as I dropped the chain. There was still more inside: a big silver bowl was piled with smaller ones.

I was confused, and astonished. This was greater booty than a warrior, however successful in battle, could hope to gain in a score of campaigns. And it must have lain here for more than a hundred years. No one owned it unless the Spirits did, and being insubstantial they could have little use for it. It was mine and I was rich – richer, maybe, than my grandfather Harding.

Wariness followed on the thrill of triumph and delight. Even if I could carry all this with me it would be unwise to do so. In fact I must take very little: a couple of small pots, say. But I could mark the place and come to it whenever I wished and get what I needed. It was safer here than anywhere. This was mostly deserted land, lying close to the great ruins of the Disaster, and even if a shepherd came within sight of it he would not venture near: all country people believed in the Spirits, and feared them.

I took a small pot of gold and a plate of the same metal, no more than four inches across, and put them in my pack. I picked up a golden candlestick but replaced it. I was not going to be so stupid as to be greedy. When I was older . . . gold and silver would buy not only houses, farms, servants, but men also. I would have more followers than the Blaines and the Hardings together. And with men one had power. Enough, when the time was ripe, to take the city. And other cities.

Holding up my candle I saw a door beyond the table. I crossed the room and tried the handle. It opened easily, though creakingly.

Inside there were buckets. They were neither of wood nor metal but of that substance called plast which the ancients made and which countrymen, when they turn it up during digging, are careful to burn, washing their hands if they have touched it. It is often brightly coloured but is not painted because the colour goes right through. I saw a blue bucket and two yellow ones. All were full, heaped with bracelets and brooches and necklaces and other jewelry, of gold set with many precious stones. Here was not just riches, but wealth incalculable.

I looked further in the room. A wooden chest, three feet square and of the same height, more than half full of jewels; and a bowl, a couple of feet across, crammed to the brim and with a string of large pearls spilling over the edge. And a bed. A figure lay there.

I knew he was dead. I knew also that there is even less to fear from the dead than from the Spirits the Seer tells of. I went closer, expecting to see the gleam of bones picked white by time. But flesh still covered him – dried and darkened, pulled away from the grinning teeth and blackened at the eyeholes, but preserved. He had died in a dry summer, perhaps, and his flesh had withered instead of rotting. It sometimes happens.

His face looked mean and pinched. So would any man's whose skin had shrunk and turned to leather, but I wondered if in fact his features had changed so much. It was he who had brought the treasure here – I was sure of that. When the Disaster came and huge cities tumbled like children's play bricks – the cities so vast that a score of Winchesters could be lost within the bounds of one – most of the people, thousands times a thousand, died in them. The few that survived fled into the country to grub a living.

But he had not. He had gone back into the ruins, risking earthquake and plague and starvation, to dig for gold and silver and precious stones. They were a rich people, our ancestors, and there would be much to find. He had brought it here, load after load, to his underground storeroom. A dozen or so trinkets lay on the bed beside him, like the toys a child puts by his pillow at night, and on his wrist I saw three tiny clocks, each fastened to a gold bracelet.

How long had he lived here? Years, probably – such a haul could not have been unearthed from the ruins in any short time. And how died? Of sickness or old age? Or perhaps of hunger, having no food in reach and being unwilling to leave his treasure to hunt for some.

The Disaster had happened . . . people had died in numbers that one could not begin to imagine . . . the world had been shattered into small ugly pieces . . . and he had stayed here, counting his wealth by candlelight. He had withered until death came, then withered further. He had changed not much more than the gold. Even the rats had shunned him.

A sudden fear struck me which had nothing to do with Spirits or the dead man lying on the bed. It was rather a chill despair striking deep inside me, a sense of hopelessness biting into my heart and bones. I had a desperate need to leave this place, not because of its ghosts but because there were none. There was nothing but emptiness and desolation, and barren treasure.

I ran back to the other room. Even standing on the table the hole in the ceiling would be out of reach, but if the table were upended . . . I dragged it across to the wall, sending its heap of cobwebbed metal clattering to the ground, and, ignoring the pain in my leg, scrambled up and balanced precariously on top. I would have to leap to reach the jagged hole above me: would the broken laths take my weight or collapse? There was no point in hesitation. I leapt, felt the edge give, then clawed my way up until I reached a beam.

I straddled it for a moment. The way was open to the sky and the world outside. I had started the last few feet when I remembered something. I felt in my pack and found the golden pot and plate. I pitched them down and heard them crash in the darkness.

The day was bright now, with only a thin white steam rising from the ground and the sky clear apart from wispy cloud. I soon found the river and followed it northwards. Ten minutes later I came to a village. It would be the one, I guessed, built round the river's southernmost ford, which meant that the army was no more than two or three miles away.

But the village itself was enough. I hurried, limping, towards it, filled with joy at the sound of a dog's barking, the sight of smoking chimneys. At the outskirts a man drew water from a well. He wore a servant's clothes and as he turned to me I saw that one eye was lower in his face than the other, with a cast in it, and that his right arm was stiff and crooked.

He bowed his head, saying: "Greetings, master."

I looked at him, not shrinking away.

I said: "Greetings, brother."

HURLED INTO SPACE

FROM *ROUND THE MOON*

JULES VERNE

Jules Verne, who was French and lived from 1825 to 1905, was the father of modern science fiction. He was also one of the first writers to imagine the means by which men might make the journey to the moon. In Round the Moon *he has his three travellers — it hardly seems right to call them astronauts — being shot into space inside a projectile like an enormous bullet, fired from an immense gun. Together with the dogs they are taking with them, they prepare for blast-off.*

ONCE TEN O'CLOCK had struck, Michel Ardan, Barbicane and Nicholl said their farewells to the many friends they would soon be leaving behind. The two dogs, whose fate it would be to acclimatise their species to conditions on the moon, were already inside the projectile. The three travellers approached the opening of the huge iron tube and were lowered by crane to the missile's cone-shaped covering. There, through another opening, they passed into the interior of the aluminium craft. The crane was withdrawn and the last scaffolding was at once cleared away from the mouth of the Columbiad.

The moment they were inside, Nicholl closed the opening with a powerful plate that was screwed down from within. Other close-fitting plates covered the lens-shaped glass of the skylights. The travellers, hermetically sealed in their metal prison, were in complete darkness.

"And now, my dear friends," said Michel Ardan, "let us make ourselves at home. Myself, I am a domesticated person, and I know how to make the best of any lodgings in which I chance to find myself. First, let us have a light. It wasn't for moles that they invented gas!"

So saying, the cheerful fellow struck a match on the sole of his boot and applied it to the burner of the gas-container, in which was stored, under enormous pressure, enough carbonised hydrogen to light and heat the compartment for 144 hours, or six days and nights.

Once the gas was lighted, the projectile was seen to resemble a comfortable room, with padded walls; it was furnished with circular divans, and the roof was dome-shaped.

The objects inside the compartment, instruments, weapons and tools, were securely fastened to withstand the shock of take-off. Every possible precaution had been taken to ensure the success of this daring experiment.

Michel Ardan carried out a thorough inspection and declared himself satisfied.

"It is a prison," he said, "but a travelling prison . . . You are smiling, Barbicane! You are thinking some private thought? Are you saying to yourself that this prison might be our coffin? So let it be! I would not change it for Mahomet's, which merely hangs in space without moving!"

While Michel Ardan was holding forth in this manner, Barbicane and Nicholl were making their final preparations.

By Nicholl's chronometer it was 10.20 p.m. when the sealing of the three travellers in their projectile was completed. This chronometer was synchronised to the tenth of a second with that of the engineer, Murchison. Barbicane looked at it.

"My friends," he said, "it is twenty past ten. At thirteen minutes to eleven Murchison will fire the Columbiad; at that moment precisely we shall leave our planet. So we still have twenty-seven minutes on earth."

"Twenty-six minutes and thirteen seconds," said the methodical Nicholl.

"Very well," said Michel Ardan, amiably. "We can do a great deal in twenty-six minutes. We might discuss important moral or political problems – and even solve them! Twenty-six minutes well used are worth more than twenty-six years of idleness. A few seconds in the life of a Pascal or a Newton have more value than the whole existence of a multitude of idiots."

"And what do you conclude from that, you indefatigable talker?" asked President Barbicane.

"I conclude that we have twenty-six minutes," said Ardan.

"Only twenty-four!" said Nicholl.

"Twenty-four, then, if you wish, gallant captain," said Ardan; "twenty-four minutes, during which we might consider –"

"Michel," said Barbicane, "during our journey we shall have all the time in the world to consider the most profound questions. Now we must think of starting."

"Are we not ready?"

"Certainly we are. But there are still precautions we must take if we are to deaden the first shock as much as possible."

"Have we not cushions of water, sandwiched between movable partitions, that are resilient enough to give us all the protection we require?"

"I hope so, Michel," said Barbicane, gently; "but I am not absolutely sure."

"Ah, the comical fellow!" Michel Ardan exclaimed. "He *hopes*! He is not absolutely sure! And he waits until we are securely shut in before he makes this disgraceful confession! I demand to be let out!"

"How?" asked Barbicane.

"Well," said Michel Ardan, "it certainly would be difficult. We are in the train, and in twenty-four minutes we shall hear the guard's whistle."

"Twenty!" said Nicholl.

The three travellers looked at one another for some seconds. Then they examined closely all the objects that were imprisoned with them.

"Everything is in its proper place!" said Barbicane. "The question now is where should we put ourselves so that we can best endure the shock of take-off. The positions we take up are important, too – we must prevent the blood from rushing too violently to our heads."

"That is true," said Nicholl.

"In that case," said Michel Ardan, always prepared to suit

the action to the word, "we will stand on our heads like clowns at a circus."

"No," said Barbicane; "let us rather lie on our sides. We shall resist the shock better like that. When the projectile is fired it will matter very little whether we are inside or in front."

"It cheers me up to know it matters very little," said Michel Ardan.

"Do you agree with my suggestion, Nicholl?" said Barbicane.

"Absolutely," said the captain. "Thirteen and a half minutes to go."

"Nicholl is not a man at all." Michel exclaimed. "He is a walking chronometer, marking the seconds and with eight holes in —"

But his companions were no longer listening; they were making their final preparations with all the coolness in the world. They looked like two methodical travellers settling themselves for a train journey and making themselves as comfortable as they could. Indeed, one wonders what these American hearts are made of, which do not respond with a single extra beat to the approach of the most deadly danger.

Three beds had been placed in the projectile, deep and stoutly constructed. Nicholl and Barbicane positioned them in the centre of the disc that formed the movable floor of the compartment. There the three travellers were to lie down a few minutes before take-off.

Meanwhile Ardan, who could not stay still, roamed round their narrow prison like some wild creature in a cage, talking to his companions and to his dogs, Diana and Satellite – to whom he had some time before given these appropriate names.

"Up, Diana! Up, Satellite!" he cried, making them excited. "You are going to show the Selenite dogs just how well-behaved dogs from the Earth can be! You will do honour to the canine race! If ever we return, I shall bring back a cross-breed of 'moon-dogs' that will soon be all the rage!"

"If there are any dogs on the moon," said Barbicane.

"Of course there are," said Michel Ardan, "just as there are horses, cows, donkeys and hens. I will wager anything you like that we shall find some hens."

"I bet you a hundred dollars we find none," said Nicholl.

"Done, captain!" said Ardan, shaking hands with Nicholl. "By the way, though, you have already lost three bets with the President, seeing that the funds needed for our enterprise were found, the casting of the projectile was a success, and the Columbiad was loaded without mishap. That makes six thousand dollars."

"Yes," said Nicholl. "Twenty-three minutes and six seconds to eleven."

"I hear, captain! And that means that before another quarter of an hour has passed you will owe the President another nine thousand dollars – four thousand because the Columbiad will not burst, and five thousand because the projectile will rise higher than six miles into the air."

"I have the money," said Nicholl, patting his coat pocket, "and I shall be only too glad to pay it over."

"Well, Nicholl, I see you are an orderly fellow – something I could never be! But let me tell you that your series of bets can be of no earthly benefit to you!"

"Why?"

"Because if you win the first, the Columbiad will have burst, and the projectile with it, and Barbicane will not be there to pay you."

"My wager is deposited with the Baltimore Bank," said Barbicane simply; "and if Nicholl isn't there to receive the money, it will go to his heirs."

"What amazingly practical men you are!" cried Michel Ardan. "I admire you as much as I fail to understand you!"

"Eighteen minutes to eleven," said Nicholl.

"Only five minutes to go," said Barbicane.

"Yes, five little minutes!" said Michel Ardan. "And we are imprisoned at the bottom of a cannon 900 feet long, together with 400,000 pounds of gun-cotton, the equivalent of more than 1,600,000 pounds of ordinary powder! And friend Murchison, with his chronometer in his hand, his eye on the dial and his finger on the electric button, is counting the seconds before he hurls us into the planetary regions!"

"Enough, Michel, enough!" said Barbicane in a grave voice. "Let us prepare ourselves. A few seconds only separate us from a supreme moment. Your hands, my friends."

"Yes," cried Michel Ardan, more moved than he cared to appear.

The three daring companions shook hands.

"God help us!" said the President.

Michel Ardan and Nicholl lay down on their beds in the middle of the floor.

"Thirteen minutes to eleven," murmured the captain.

Twenty seconds to go! Barbicane quickly put out the gas and lay down beside the others.

The profound silence was broken only by the chronometer as it beat out the seconds.

Suddenly a fearful shock was felt, and the projectile, impelled by 6,000,000,000 litres of gas created by the sudden combustion of the pyroxyle, rose into space.

GOODBYE TO THE MOON

FROM *CRISIS ON CONSHELF TEN*

MONICA HUGHES

Kepler Masterman is fifteen: he was born on the Moon, of which his father is the Governor. And now, for the first time, he is about to fly from that familiar place, the Moon, to that place excitingly unknown, the Earth.

I SAT IN the darkened viewing room of the space station and looked out at Earth. It was strangely familiar to me. The photograph of the blue globe with its whip-cream swirls of cloud hung in the Control Centre of Lunar Lab 21. There was a small copy of the same famous picture in our own living unit. To my mother and father it had meant home.

What was this Earth to me? It was a shining silver disc, waxing from crescent to full, and waning back again to crescent, that traversed the skies of our long lunar nights. It was the song my mother sang to me, the first child born on Moon:

Earth-shine, Earth-bright, Grant the wish I wish tonight.

But that was long, long ago. Mother had been dead for five years, and I, Kepler Masterman, son of Moon Governor, was actually going to Earth myself. Already I was over the first hurdle, the wearisome three day journey on the old beat-up Moon-ferry to the space station.

It was great to stretch my legs again and enjoy the lowgrav of the station's slow spin after the weight of the moon-rocket's acceleration. I looked down at Earth, so close I felt I could reach out and touch. What was down there? . . . The Sphinx . . . the Taj Mahal . . . Skyscrapers. All the fantastic things I'd read about. I looked at my watch. Fifteen minutes to wait.

Restlessly I left the viewing room and glided down the long passageway to the hub of the space station. In the VIP lounge I could see Father, surrounded by reporters. Time for one last goodbye to Moon.

Down the passage to the right here. The view room was empty, and I slid into a couch in the centre front row. The room was dark and the window was set in an angle that fooled the eye. It was as if nothing separated me from the black infinity of space and from Moon. It was so small now, my Moon, no bigger than the silver identidisc on the chain around my neck.

My eyes picked out the familiar features. The terminator, that razor-edge between night and day, arced down through the Ocean of Storms. The oblique sunlight etched clearly in black shadow the huge circle of Copernicus, and, to its left, right on the edge of the terminator, I could see Kepler, the crater in which Lunar Lab was built. Home! Down there a new Moon-day was just starting. The viewing ports of the Labs and of the living units would automatically darken as the brilliant rays of the sun stabbed down white-hard against the rocks of the crater. The heat-exchange units would slowly adjust from two weeks of warming up the buildings to cooling them, as for the next fifteen days the sun would shine down on Lunar Lab 21.

Down there at home the kids would be getting ready for the party. There'd always been a party at sunrise, ever since I could remember, and I was the oldest kid on Moon. The adults used to tease us sometimes . . . "Imagine having a party every *day*!" But, heck, it was only twelve or thirteen times a year, and there was something special about the sunlight creeping so slowly across the surface of Moon, striking the peaks of the Apennines, sending shadows chasing across the Sinus Aestium, each Earth-day a little closer, until finally the two long weeks of night were over, and we were bathed in sunlight again. The astronomers hated daytime, except for the solar experts. They couldn't see the stars and had to stay in their rooms catching up on their paperwork. But everyone else loved it, especially the kids.

I sighed and thought of Ann. Wonder who'd be taking her to the party? We'd stood at the air-lock to say goodbye. Ann had been crying and her eyes were red. But she was as beautiful as ever. There had been an awful lump in my throat as I blurted out the words.

"I'll be seeing you, Ann."

"Oh, Kepler, take care of yourself."

"Sure. You too, Ann. I'll write, I promise."

It was a terrible farewell. I'd worked out ahead of time exactly what I was going to say. It was terrific. It'd have bowled her over. But standing there by the air-lock I'd forgotten it all.

I squirmed at the memory and hoped that Ann wouldn't remember and laugh. Well, at least I could write. I knew I couldn't expect letters from Ann. Letter rates to Earth were crippling – so was the cost of everything that had to make the 240,000 mile haul. But I could write to Ann. That was one advantage of having the Lunar Governor as Father. I could slip my letters into the diplomatic bag and they would go rocketing to Moon with no questions asked. But six months away from home . . . gosh; I was going to miss her. *That* was the disadvantage of having a Governor for Father.

The door swung open behind me, letting in a shaft of light and a babble of excited voices. There was a waft of exotic perfume. Real French perfume! The ferry from Earth must have arrived. These would be passengers on Moon Safari. This was a trip only for the very, very wealthy. In fact the tourist complex on the Sea of Serenity helped pay for some of the research expenses that Moon administration was unable to wring from the reluctant cashbox of Earth.

I slipped out of the suddenly crowded room and down the passage to the central concourse. Father was standing there. There were last minute goodbyes.

"Good luck, George."

"We're counting on you, Governor!"

"See you in six months, at the latest."

I walked beside him, trying to copy his casual stroll. I wasn't about to look like some country Rube even if it was my first Earth trip. But my first sight of the Earth-ferry threw me and my jaw dropped. It was magnificent, three times as big as our beat-up old Moon-ferries with their huge cargo holds and dingy cramped passenger quarters. Yet we had had to endure the lunar trip for three long days, and this was only going to take about three hours.

"Is everything on Earth this fancy?" I whispered to Father, as I snuggled down into the deep plush of my contour seat, and buckled my harness round me.

"Pretty much so – in the parts of the world you'll be seeing, anyway. It's a far cry from home, isn't it?"

Was it ever! I tried to imagine our living unit with a deep blue pile carpet and walls of cream stippled with gold, instead of the standard issue green vinyl floor and plastic-coated steel walls. When I was a kid I was always roaming into the wrong unit. They were all identical, and there just wasn't the money to ferry up from Earth the sort of things that would have made them look homey . . .

. . . The ferry shivered delicately and then moved slowly out of its holding dock. I could feel my body pressing gently against the padded couch as the ferry surrendered itself to Earth-grav. It was amazingly quiet and comfortable. I'd hardly slept on the trip down from Moon, and now, in spite of myself, I found my eyes shutting.

It seemed only a few minutes before Father's voice woke me. "You're a pretty blasé traveller, Kepler! But you mustn't miss this sight. We're just turning into Earth orbit. Look!"

I craned my neck eagerly and looked through the port. I recognized the narrow spindle of central America, and then the steely shimmer of the Atlantic lay beneath us. It went on and on.

"The planet's all water!" I gasped.

"Seven-tenths of it is," Father agreed.

"But . . . but. Oh, wow!" It was feeble, but what words could I have for it? A world that was seven-tenths *water*! Why, on Moon, water was harder to get than oxygen, much harder. Breathing was free. You could breathe as deeply and as often as you wished. Now that the hydroponic gardens were going we didn't have to pay for our oxygen any more. But water was something else. Every ounce of it was worth its weight in Moon minerals. Dirt was removed by electrostatic filters in the labs and living units. Washing was a luxury and drinking a special delight.

There was no free water on Moon. Every ounce we used was extracted in the refinement of the ores we sent down to Earth. And the mining companies charged us for it — every drop! I had grown up thinking water was the most precious stuff in the Universe. Now with my own eyes I could see that Earth was covered with the stuff — slopping over with it.

We orbited across North Africa and Arabia. From my port I could see the island-spangled blueness of the Indian Ocean. Then the Pacific. I felt suddenly tired and a little sick. What sort of a place was this Earth and what were its people like? Half a world made of water, and yet they had charged us for every single cup. I shut my eyes and turned away from the port.

"You feeling groggy?" Father's voice was sympathetic.

"They're starting their braking orbit, and I guess you'll really notice the weight difference. Don't worry. It'll get worse before it gets better. But it will get better. Just hang on!"

To the Earth passengers from the space station I suppose the discomforts were minimal. Their apparent weight increased to double and momentarily three times their normal weight. I had not realised until this moment what my birthright of one-sixth Earth weight was going to mean when I tried to return 'home'. It was like a barrier separating me from all these other people. Already I weighed six times my normal weight. As the braking continued it increased to twelve times, to . . . The weight on my chest . . . I couldn't breathe. I felt as if my brain was going to burst.

When I came back to my senses the enormous pressure had lifted. I felt heavy and very tired. I lifted my head and looked blurrily around. We had landed! There was a bustle of unstrapping harnesses, collecting belongings. I struggled with my own safety straps, and Father leaned over to help me. The expression on his face told me I didn't look good.

"Lie still, Kepler. You've had a nose-bleed. I'll get a stewardess to help."

"I'm okay, Father." My tongue felt thick and the words were blurry. The stewardess hurried over. She bent down to wash my face.

"I can do it," I muttered thickly, trying to take the cloth away from her.

"You just lie still, sonny. I'm just going to get you an icepack. You really took the 'Gs' badly. You'll have two beautiful shiners in the morning."

Sonny! How old did she think I was, anyway? Two black eyes . . . oh, brother! That was really starting out on the right foot. Look out, Earth. Here comes Kepler Masterman – on a banana skin!

She glided back with the icepack. How could she move so lightly on this heavy planet, I wondered. She looked no heavier than a grain of moondust.

She spoke to my father. "Governor, the Press and TV are waiting for you. Are you ready to leave the ferry yet?" "Oh, sure. I'll come right away." He swung himself up from his couch and stretched. He was a big man, my father, and muscular. I wondered if I'd ever catch up. I was at the weedy stage, and in spite of secret body-building in my own room I wasn't making much headway.

"Strange feeling going up to 170 pounds again. Don't think I like it much. Kepler, lie still and take your time. I'm sure this young lady will look after you."

I watched his broad back down the aisle and through the hatch, and then I took off the icepack and swung my legs down to the floor. My head throbbed a bit, but it wasn't too bad. Standing was tougher, and walking was a nightmare of wading through glue. I gritted my teeth and practised, one foot and then the other, up and down the aisle, holding on to the seat backs for support. Six months on this planet. How was I ever going to make out? I saw the stewardess watching me from the galley door. I wished she'd go away, but when she saw I'd seen her she came down the aisle towards me.

"I could get you a wheelchair," she volunteered. "This low-grav syndrome can be a problem. It's happened before, you know, though I guess you're the first person who's never experienced Earth-weight in his life."

"I'm going to be fine, thanks. It just takes a little practice, that's all."

"Of course. Perhaps you'd like to tidy up before you leave?"

I took her hint and plodded back down the aisle to the washroom. Good grief, I was a disaster area! I took off my jacket – how crudely cut it looked in comparison with the Earth fashions I'd seen on the ferry, and what rough material. Then I washed the rest of the blood off my face and combed my hair, what there was of it. It looked like a convict cut by Earth standards, but it would grow. There were red smudges under my eyes, but the shiners the stewardess had promised hadn't shown up yet. I put on my jacket and plodded down to the exit hatch. I hesitated, my hand on the ramp rail, looking at the crowd of exotically dressed reporters, cameramen and casual bystanders milling around my father. It really was a new world down there at the end of the ramp.

"Good luck," the stewardess said softly. She wasn't a bad sort, really, only a bit old to understand. I managed a smile, swallowed and walked down the ramp to join my father. I was drowned in a storm of voices. How loudly these Earth people talked, as if they were constantly trying to shout each other down.

"Governor, would you say the differences between Earth

and Moon people are irreconcilable?"

"I certainly would not. On the contrary I am convinced that with a clearer understanding of our problem, the differences between us will be settled amicably."

"What do you intend to do if the U.N. vote goes against you?"

"I'm not even considering that possibility at the moment."

"Governor, how long do you intend to spend on Earth this trip?"

"I anticipate that it may take as long as six months to settle our differences, though of course we could strike lucky . . ."

"One last question, Governor. Now you are back on Earth again will you tell our listeners – which is really home to you, Earth or Moon?"

"That's a difficult question to answer. All my cultural ties are with Earth. But, like all immigrants who flocked to the New World and shaped it into a nation, I guess I must say that it is in this Newer World, Moon, that my present and future lie. My son was born there. My wife was buried there. My work is there. Yes, gentlemen, it is good to be back on Earth. But Moon is home!"

He saw me standing jammed among the reporters and casually gave me his arm. We walked together across the sun-splashed concrete of the landing pad. The sun was gently warm on my body and our shadows ran out ahead of us, soft, muzzy-edged. I looked up. The sky was a delicate blue with fluffy cumulus clouds, just like the ones in my old video tapes. They sailed gracefully across the sky, unbelievably beautiful. A sudden white shape plunged and screeched. I jumped and clutched Father's arm.

"What was that? . . . A bird?"

"Yes, Kepler. A sea-gull."

I walked along, breathing real air, not the canned stuff. It was strange being out of doors without a space-suit, scary but exciting. It looked as if Earth was going to be fun. If only my legs didn't ache so . . .

"Is it far to the magnetrain, Father?"

"Hang on, son. It's right ahead."

Once aboard with my feet up I didn't feel so much of a country cousin. The magnetrain had been developed on Moon, where the absence of any atmosphere had precluded the use of conventional jet, hovercraft or internal combustion engines. Up there we had perfected the magnetic lift system of propulsion and our trains networked the lunar surface with silent pollution-free speeds of 500 miles an hour.

The idea had been enthusiastically adopted by an ecology-conscious Earth, and one of the items on my father's agenda was to negotiate an acknowledgement in terms of royalties of the Lunar discovery.

I lay back and thought of the pyramids and the Taj Mahal, the temples of Angkor Wat and the mysterious jungle buildings of the Incas. Would six months be time enough to see it all?

THE SHOT FROM THE MOON

FROM *ISLANDS IN THE SKY*

ARTHUR C. CLARKE

*Roy Malcolm is a sort of trainee in space. He is learning
what is involved in orbiting the Earth, five hundred miles
above it, in a space-station. Some things that happen are
arranged beforehand, for the benefit of learners like Roy. So
an imaginary meteor makes a hole in the skin of the space-
station, and the apprentices have to learn what to do when
that happens. They also encounter Cuthbert, a space monster
rather like an octopus, who turns out to be less terrifying than
he seems. But some of the problems that arise are real
enough, like one that occurs when the spaceship they are on,
heading from the Moon to Earth, turns out to be travelling in
quite another direction.*

"COMMANDER DOYLE," SAID the pilot, in a very thin
voice. "Will you come here a minute?" The Commander
stirred in his bunk.

"Confound it – I was nearly asleep!"

"I'm sorry, but – well, there's been an accident. We're –
we're in an escape orbit."

"What!"

The roar woke up everyone else. With a mighty heave the Commander left his bunk and headed for the control desk. There was a rapid conference with the unhappy pilot; then the Commander said, "Get me the nearest Relay Station. I'm taking over."

"What's happened?" I whispered to Tim Benton.

"I think I know," said Tim, "but wait a minute before we jump to conclusions."

It was almost a quarter of an hour before anyone bothered to explain things to me – a quarter of an hour of furious activity, radio calls, and lightning calculations. Then Norman Powell, who like me had nothing to do but watch, took pity on my ignorance.

"This ship's got a curse on it," he said in disgust. "The pilot's made the one navigation error you'd think was impossible. He should have cut our speed by point nine miles a second. Instead, he applied power in exactly the wrong direction – we've *gained* speed by that amount. So instead of falling Earthwards, we're heading out into space."

Even to me, it seemed hard to imagine that anyone could make such an extraordinary mistake. Later, I discovered that it was one of those things – like landing an aircraft with wheels up – that isn't as difficult to do as it sounds. Aboard a spaceship in free orbit, there's no way of telling in what direction and at what speed you're moving. Everything has to be done by instruments and calculations – and if at a certain stage a minus sign is taken for a plus, then it's easy to point the ship in exactly the wrong direction before applying power.

Of course, one is supposed to make other checks to prevent such mistakes. Somehow they hadn't worked this time, or the pilot hadn't applied them. It wasn't until a long time later that we found the full reason. The jammed oxygen valve, not the unhappy pilot, was the real culprit. I'd been the only one who had actually fainted, but the others had all been suffering from oxygen starvation. It's a very dangerous complaint, because you don't realize that there's anything wrong with you. In fact it's rather like being drunk: you can be making all sorts of stupid mistakes, yet feel that you're right on top of your job.

But it was not much use finding why the accident had happened. The problem now was – what should we do next?

The extra speed we'd been given was just enough to put us into an escape orbit. In other words, we were travelling so fast that the Earth could never pull us back. We were heading out into space, somewhere beyond the orbit of the Moon – we wouldn't know our exact path until we got HAVOC to work it out for us. Commander Doyle had radioed our position and velocity, and now we had to wait for further instructions.

The situation was serious, but not hopeless. We still had a considerable amount of fuel – the reserve intended for the approach to the Inner Station. If we used it now, we could at least prevent ourselves flying away from Earth, but we should then be travelling in a new orbit that might take us nowhere near any of the space-stations. Whatever happened, we *had* to get fresh fuel from somewhere – and as quickly as possible. The short-range ship in which we were travelling wasn't designed for long excursions into space, and carried only a limited oxygen supply. We had enough for about a hundred hours: if help couldn't reach us by that time, it would be just too bad ...

It's a funny thing, but though I was now in real danger for the first time, I didn't feel half as frightened as I did when we were caught by Cuthbert, or when the 'meteor' holed the classroom. Somehow, this seemed different. We had several days' breathing-space — literally! — before the crisis would be upon us. And we all had such confidence in Commander Doyle that we were sure he could get us out of this mess.

Though we couldn't really appreciate it at the time, there was certainly something ironic about the fact that we'd have been quite safe if we'd stuck to the 'Morning Star' and not ultra-cautiously decided to go home on another ship ...

We had to wait for nearly fifteen minutes before the computing staff on the Inner Station worked out our new orbit and radioed it back to us. Commander Doyle plotted our path and we all craned over his shoulder to see what course the ship was going to follow.

"We're heading for the Moon," he said, tracing out the dotted line with his finger. "We'll pass its orbit in about forty hours, near enough for its gravitational field to have quite an effect. If we like to use some rocket braking, we can let it capture us."

"Wouldn't that be a good idea? At least it would stop us heading out into space."

The Commander rubbed his chin thoughtfully.

"I don't know," he said. "It depends if there are any ships on the Moon that can come up to us."

"Can't we land on the Moon ourselves, near one of the settlements?" asked Norman.

"No – we've not enough fuel for the descent. The motors aren't powerful enough, anyway – you ought to know that."

Norman subsided, and the cabin was filled with a long, thoughtful silence that began to get on my nerves. I wished I could help with some bright ideas, but it wasn't likely they'd be any better than Norman's.

"The trouble is," said the Commander at last, "that there are so many factors involved. There are several *possible* solutions to our problem. What we want to find is the *most economical* one. It's going to cost a fortune if we have to call up a ship from the Moon, just to match our speed and transfer a few tons of fuel. That's the obvious, brute-force answer."

It was a relief to know that there *was* an answer. That was really all that I wanted to hear. Someone else would have to worry about the bill.

Suddenly the pilot's face lit up. He had been sunk in gloom until now and hadn't contributed a word to the conversation.

"I've got it!" he said. "We should have thought of it before! What's wrong with using the launcher down in Hipparchus? That should be able to shoot us up some fuel without any trouble – as far as one can tell from this chart."

The conversation then grew very animated and very technical, and I was rapidly left behind. Ten minutes later the general gloom in the cabin began to disperse, so I guessed that some satisfactory conclusion had been reached. When the discussion had died away, and all the radio calls had been made, I got Tim into a corner and threatened to keep bothering until he explained exactly what was going on.

"Surely, Roy," he said, "you know about the Hipparchus launcher?"

"Isn't it that magnetic thing that shoots fuel tanks up to rockets orbiting the Moon?"

"Of course: it's an electro-magnetic track about five miles long, running east and west across the crater Hipparchus. They chose that spot because it's near the centre of the Moon's disc, and the fuel refineries aren't far away. Ships waiting to be refuelled get into an orbit round the Moon, and at the right time they shoot up the containers into the same orbit. The ship's got to do a bit of manoeuvring by rocket power to 'home' on the tank, but it's much cheaper than doing the whole job by rockets."

"What happens to the empty tanks?"

"That depends on the launching speed. Sometimes they crash back on the Moon – after all, there's plenty of room for them to come down without doing any harm! But usually they're given lunar escape velocity, so they just get lost in space. There's even more room out *there* . . ."

"I see – we're going near enough to the Moon for a fuel tank to be shot out to us."

"Yes: they're doing the calculations now. Our orbit will pass behind the Moon, about five thousand miles above the surface. They'll match our speed as accurately as they can with the launcher, and we'll have to do the rest under our own power: it'll mean using some of our fuel, of course – but the investment will be worth it!"

"And when will all this happen?"

"In about forty hours: we're waiting for the exact figures now."

I was probably the only one who felt really pleased with the prospect, now that I knew we were reasonably safe. To the others, this was a tedious waste of time – but it was going to give me an opportunity of seeing the Moon at close quarters. This was certainly far more than I could have dared hope when I left Earth: the Inner Station already seemed a long way behind me . . .

Hour by hour Earth dwindled and the Moon grew larger in the sky ahead. There was very little to do, apart from routine checks of the instruments and regular radio calls to the various space-stations and the lunar base. Most of the time was spent sleeping and playing cards, but once I was given a chance of speaking to Mom and Pop, way back on Earth. They sounded a bit worried, and for the first time I realized that we were probably making headlines. However, I think I made it clear that I was enjoying myself and there was no real need for any alarm.

All the necessary arrangements had been made, and there was nothing to do but wait until we swept past the Moon and made our appointment with the fuel container. Though I had often watched the Moon through telescopes, both from Earth and from the Inner Station, it was a very different matter to see the great plains and mountains with my own unaided eyes.

We were now so close that all the larger craters were easily visible, along the band dividing night from day. The line of sunrise had just passed the centre of the disc, and it was early dawn down there in Hipparchus, where they were preparing for our rescue. I asked permission to borrow the ship's telescope, and peered down into the great crater.

It seemed that I was hanging in space only fifty miles above the Moon. Hipparchus completely filled the field of vision – it was impossible to take it all in at one glance. The sunlight was slanting over the ruined walls of the crater, casting mile-long pools of inky shadow. Here and there upthrust peaks caught the first light of the dawn, and blazed like beacons in the darkness all around them.

And there were other lights in the crater shadows – lights arranged in tiny, geometric patterns. I was looking down on one of the lunar settlements: hidden from me in the darkness were the great chemical plants, the pressurized domes, the space-ports and the power stations that drove the launching track. In a few hours they would be clearly visible as the Sun rose above the mountains – but by then we should have passed behind the Moon and the Earthward side would be hidden from us.

And then I saw it – a thin bar of light stretching in a dead straight line across the darkened plain. I was looking at the floodlights of the launching track, ranged like the lamps along an arterial road. By their illumination, space-suited engineers would be checking the great electromagnets and seeing that the cradle ran freely in its guides. The fuel tank would be waiting at the head of the track, already loaded and ready to be placed on the cradle when the time arrived. If it had been daylight down there, perhaps I could have seen the actual launch. There would have been a tiny speck racing along the track, moving more and more swiftly as the generators poured their power into the magnets. It would leave the end of the launcher at a speed of over five thousand miles an hour – too fast for the Moon ever to pull it back. As it travelled almost horizontally, the surface of the Moon would curve away beneath it and it would swoop out into space – to meet us, if all went well, three hours later.

I think the most impressive moment of all my adventures came when the ship passed behind the Moon, and I saw with my own eyes the land that had remained hidden from human sight until the coming of the rocket. It was true that I had seen many films and photographs of the Moon's other side – and it was also true that it was very much the same as the visible face. Yet somehow the thrill remained. I thought of all the astronomers who had spent their lives charting the Moon, and had never seen the land over which I was now passing. What would they have given for the opportunity that had now come to me – and come quite by chance, without any real effort on my part!

I had almost forgotten Earth when Tim Benton drew my attention to it again. It was sinking swiftly towards the lunar horizon: the Moon was rising up to eclipse it as we swept along in our great arc. A blinding blue-green crescent – the South Polar cap – almost too brilliant to look upon, the reflection of the Sun forming a pool of fire in the Pacific Ocean – that was my home, now a quarter of a million miles away. I watched it drop behind the cruel lower peaks until only the faint, misty rim was visible: then even this disappeared. The Sun was still with us – but Earth had gone. Until this moment it had always been with us in the sky, part of the background of things. Now I had only Sun, Moon and stars.

The fuel container was already on its way up to meet us. It had been launched an hour ago, and we had been told by radio that it was proceeding on the correct orbit. The Moon's gravitational field would curve its path and we would pass within a few hundred miles of it. Our job then was to match speeds by careful use of our remaining fuel and, when we had coupled our ship up to the tank, pump across its contents. Then we could turn for home and the empty container would coast on out into space, to join the rest of the debris circulating in the Solar System.

"But just suppose," I said anxiously to Norman Powell, "that they score a direct hit on us! After all, the whole thing's rather like shooting a gun at a target. And *we're* the target."

Norman laughed.

"It'll be moving very slowly when it comes up to us, and we'll spot it on our radar when it's a long way off. So there's no danger of collision. By the time it is really close, we'll have matched speeds and if we bump it'll be about as violent as two snowflakes meeting head-on."

That was reassuring, though I still didn't really like the idea of this projectile from the Moon tearing up at us through space . . .

We picked up the signals from the fuel container when it was still a thousand miles away – not with our radar, but thanks to the tiny radio beacon that all these missiles carried to aid their detection. After this I kept out of the way while Commander Doyle and the pilot made our rendezvous in space. It was a delicate operation, this jockeying of a ship until it matched the course of the still-invisible projectile. Our fuel reserves were too slim to permit any more mistakes, and everyone breathed a great sigh of relief when the stubby, shining cylinder was hanging beside us.

The transfer took only about ten minutes, and when our pumps had finished their work the Earth had emerged from behind the Moon's shield. It seemed a good omen: we were once more masters of the situation – and in sight of home again.

I was watching the radar screen – because no one else wanted to use it – when we turned on the motors again. The empty fuel container, which had now been uncoupled, seemed to fall slowly astern. Actually, of course, it was we who were falling back – checking our speed to return Earthwards. The fuel capsule would go shooting on out into space, thrown away now that its task was completed.

The extreme range of our radar was about five hundred miles, and I watched a bright spot representing the fuel container drift slowly towards the edge of the screen. It was the only object near enough to produce an echo. The volume of space which our beams were sweeping probably contained quite a number of meteors, but they were far too small to produce a visible signal. Yet there was something fascinating about watching even this almost empty screen – empty, that is, apart from an occasional sparkle of light caused by electrical interference. It made me visualize the thousand-mile-diameter globe at whose centre we were travelling. Nothing of any size could enter that globe without our invisible radio fingers detecting it and giving the alarm.

We were now safely back on course, no longer racing out into space. Commander Doyle had decided not to return directly to the Inner Station, because our oxygen reserve was getting low. Instead, we would home on one of the three Relay Stations, twenty-two thousand miles above the Earth. The ship could be re-provisioned there before we continued the last lap of our journey.

I was just about to switch off the radar screen when I saw a faint spark of light at extreme range. It vanished a second later as our beam moved into another sector of space, and I waited until it had swept through the complete cycle, wondering if I'd been mistaken. Were there any other spaceships around here? It was quite possible, of course.

There was no doubt about it – the spark appeared again, in the same position. I knew how to work the scanner controls, and stopped the beam sweeping, so that it locked on to the distant echo. It was just under five hundred miles away, moving very slowly with respect to us. I looked at it thoughtfully for a few seconds, and then called Tim. It was probably not important enough to bother the Commander. However, there was just the chance that it was a really large meteor, and they were always worth investigating. One that gave an echo this size would be much too big to bring home, but we might be able to chip bits off it for souvenirs – if we matched speed with it, of course.

Tim started the scanner going as soon as I handed over the controls. He thought I'd picked up our discarded fuel container again – which annoyed me since it showed little faith in my commonsense. But he soon saw that it was in a completely different part of the sky and his scepticism vanished.

"It must be a spaceship," he said, "though it doesn't seem a large enough echo for that. We'll soon find out – if it's a ship, it'll be carrying a radio beacon."

He turned our receiver to the beacon frequency, but without result. There were a few ships at great distances in other parts of the sky, but nothing as close as this.

Norman had now joined us and was looking over Tim's shoulder.

"If it's a meteor," he said, "let's hope it's a nice lump of platinum or something equally valuable. Then we can retire for life."

"Hey!" I exclaimed, "I found it!"

"I don't think that counts. You're not on the crew and shouldn't be here anyway."

"Don't worry," said Tim, "no one's ever found anything except iron in meteors – in any quantity, that is. The most you can expect to run across out here is a chunk of nickel-steel, probably so tough that you won't even be able to saw off a piece as a souvenir."

By now we had worked out the course of the object, and discovered that it would pass within twenty miles of us. If we wished to make contact, we'd have to change our velocity by about two hundred miles an hour – not much, but it would waste some of our hard-won fuel and the Commander certainly wouldn't allow it, if it was merely a question of satisfying our curiosity.

"How big would it have to be," I asked, "to produce an echo this bright?"

"You can't tell," said Tim. "It depends what it's made of – and the way it's pointing. A spaceship *could* produce a signal as small as that, if we were only seeing it end-on."

"I think I've found it," said Norman suddenly. "And it *isn't* a meteor. You have a look."

He had been searching with the ship's telescope, and I took his place at the eyepiece, getting there just ahead of Tim. Against a background of faint stars a roughly cylindrical object, brilliantly lit by the sunlight, was very slowly revolving in space. Even at first glance I could see it was artificial. When I had watched it turn through a complete revolution, I could see that it was streamlined and had a pointed nose. It looked much more like an old-time artillery shell than a modern rocket. The fact that it was streamlined meant that it couldn't be an empty fuel container from the launcher in Hipparchus: the tanks it shot up were plain, stubby cylinders, since streamlining was no use on the airless Moon.

Commander Doyle stared through the telescope for a long time when we called him over. Finally, to my joy, he remarked: "Whatever it is, we'd better have a look at it and make a report. We can spare the fuel and it will only take a few minutes."

Our ship spun round in space as we began to make the course-correction. The rocket fired for a few seconds, our new path was rechecked, and the rockets operated again. After several shorter bursts, we had come to within a mile of the mysterious object and began to edge towards it under the gentle impulse of the steering jets alone. Through all these manoeuvres it was impossible to use the telescope, so when I next saw my discovery it was only a hundred yards beyond our port, very gently approaching us.

It was artificial all right, and a rocket of some kind. What it was doing out here near the Moon we could only guess, and several theories were put forward. Since it was only about ten feet long, it might be one of the automatic reconnaissance missiles sent out in the early days of space-flight. Commander Doyle didn't think this likely: as far as he knew, they'd all been accounted for. Besides, it seemed to have none of the radio and TV equipment such missiles would carry.

It was painted a very bright red — an odd colour, I thought, for anything in space. There was some lettering on the side — apparently in English, though I couldn't make out the words at this distance. As the projectile slowly revolved, a black pattern on a white background came into view, but went out of sight before I could interpret it. I waited until it came into view again: by this time the little rocket had drifted considerably closer, and was now only fifty feet away.

"I don't like the look of the thing," Tim Benton said, half to himself. "That colour, for instance – red's the sign of danger."

"Don't be an old woman," scoffed Norman. "If it was a bomb or something like that, it certainly wouldn't advertise the fact."

Then the pattern I'd glimpsed before swam back into view. Even on the first sight, there had been something uncomfortably familiar about it. Now there was no longer any doubt.

Clearly painted on the side of the slowly approaching missile was the symbol of Death – the skull and crossbones.

THE FUN THEY HAD

ISAAC ASIMOV

MARGIE EVEN WROTE about it that night in her diary. On the page headed May 17, 2157, she wrote, "Today Tommy found a real book!"

It was a very old book. Margie's grandfather once said that when he was a little boy *his* grandfather told him that there was a time when all stories were printed on paper.

They turned the pages, which were yellow and crinkly, and it was awfully funny to read words that stood still instead of moving the way they were supposed to – on a screen, you know. And then, when they turned back to the page before, it had the same words on it that it had had when they read it the first time.

"Gee," said Tommy, "what a waste. When you're through with the book, you just throw it away, I guess. Our television screen must have had a million books on it and it's good for plenty more. I wouldn't throw it away."

"Same as mine," said Margie. She was eleven and hadn't seen as many textbooks as Tommy had. He was thirteen.

She said, "Where did you find it?"

"In my house." He pointed without looking, because he

was busy reading. "In the attic."

"What's it about?"

"School."

Margie was scornful. "School? What's there to write about school? I hate school."

Margie always hated school, but now she hated it more than ever. The mechanical teacher had been giving her test after test in geography and she had been doing worse and worse until her mother had shaken her head sorrowfully and sent for the County Inspector.

He was a round little man with a red face and a whole box of tools with dials and wires. He smiled at Margie and gave her an apple, then took the teacher apart. Margie had hoped he wouldn't know how to put it together again, but he knew how all right, and, after an hour or so, there it was again, large and black and ugly, with a big screen on which all the lessons were shown and the questions were asked. That wasn't so bad. The part Margie hated most was the slot where she had to put homework and test papers. She always had to write them out in a punch code they made her learn when she was six years old, and the mechanical teacher calculated the mark in no time.

The Inspector had smiled after he was finished and patted Margie's head. He said to her mother, "It's not the little girl's fault, Mrs Jones. I think the geography sector was geared a little too quick. Those things happen sometimes. I've slowed it up to an average ten-year level. Actually, the overall pattern of her progress is quite satisfactory." And he patted Margie's head again.

Margie was disappointed. She had been hoping they would take the teacher away altogether. They had once taken Tommy's teacher away for nearly a month because the history sector had blanked out completely.

So she said to Tommy, "Why would anyone write about school?"

Tommy looked at her with very superior eyes. "Because it's not our kind of school, stupid. This is the old kind of school that they had hundreds and hundreds of years ago." He added loftily, pronouncing the word carefully, "*Centuries* ago."

Margie was hurt. "Well, I don't know what kind of school they had all that time ago." She read the book over his shoulder for a while, then said, "Anyway, they had a teacher."

"Sure they had a teacher, but it wasn't a *regular* teacher. It was a man."

"A man? How could a man be a teacher?"

"Well, he just told the boys and girls things and gave them homework and asked them questions."

"A man isn't smart enough."

"Sure he is. My father knows as much as my teacher."

"He can't. A man can't know as much as a teacher."

"He knows almost as much, I betcha."

Margie wasn't prepared to dispute that. She said, "I wouldn't want a strange man in my house to teach me."

Tommy screamed with laughter. "You don't know much, Margie. The teachers didn't live in the house. They had a special building and all the kids went there."

"And all the kids learned the same thing?"

"Sure, if they were the same age."

"But my mother says a teacher has to be adjusted to fit the mind of each boy and girl it teaches and that each kid has to be taught differently."

"Just the same they didn't do it that way then. If you don't like it, you don't have to read the book."

"I didn't say I didn't like it," Margie said quickly. She wanted to read about those funny schools.

They weren't even half-finished when Margie's mother called, "Margie! School!"

Margie looked up. "Not yet, Mamma."

"Now!" said Mrs Jones. "And it's probably time for Tommy, too."

Margie said to Tommy, "Can I read the book some more with you after school?"

"Maybe," he said nonchalantly. He walked away whistling, the dusty old book tucked beneath his arm.

Margie went into the schoolroom. It was right next to her bedroom, and the mechanical teacher was on and waiting for her. It was always on at the same time every day except Saturday and Sunday, because her mother said little girls learned better if they learned at regular hours.

The screen was lit up, and it said, "Today's arithmetic lesson is on the addition of proper fractions. Please insert yesterday's homework in the proper slot."

Margie did so with a sigh. She was thinking about the old schools they had when her grandfather's grandfather was a little boy. All the kids from the whole neighbourhood came, laughing and shouting in the schoolyard, sitting together in the same schoolroom, going home together at the end of the day. They learned the same things, so they could help one another on the homework and talk about it.

And the teachers were people . . .

The mechanical teacher was flashing on the screen: "When we add the fractions $\frac{1}{2}$ and $\frac{1}{4}$ —"

Margie was thinking about how the kids must have loved it in the old days. She was thinking about the fun they had.

A Fight between Lizards at the Centre of the Earth

Jules Verne

Professor von Hardwigg, who knows all about rocks, has discovered an old document suggesting that an explorer who descended into a crater in Finland would be able to make his way to the very centre of the Earth. He sets out with his nephew, Harry, and a Finnish guide, Hans, and they do indeed find their way downwards, mile by mile, adventure by adventure, down shafts and through galleries and tunnels, to a deep ocean. They make a raft and set out to find the other side of the water. Harry keeps a diary of what happens.

SUNDAY, AUGUST 18. Nothing new to report. The same intense light as before. I can't help being afraid that it will disappear and leave us in darkness. But it is like some immense lamp and we see perfectly. The shadow of the raft stands out clearly on the surface of the water.

This sea must go on for ever. Well, it's at least as wide as the Mediterranean is long, and perhaps as wide as the Atlantic. My uncle has made several attempts to discover how deep it is by tying one of our heaviest crowbars to a cord and allowing it to run out as far as it will go. But at two hundred fathoms it still hasn't reached the bottom.

This morning, when the crowbar is dragged back on board, Hans points out some strange marks to be seen on its surface.

"*Tänder,*" he says. Of course, I don't understand him; but he opens his mouth, and closes it again, as if he were biting something, and I see what he means. "It's been bitten by *teeth!*" I cry.

No doubt about it! The marks on the iron bar are those of teeth! But what jaws the owner of such teeth must have! The bar, which is of solid iron, is almost bitten through!

Are there fearful creatures at the bottom of this sea, so close to the centre of the Earth? Will they surface? Doing what they have done to the crowbar, what would they do to our raft? Or to us?

But it is Sunday, and we try to spend a quiet and hopeful day.

Monday, August 19. I have been thinking about the great creatures that used to inhabit the surface of the Earth, the saurians! Is it possible that such hideous monsters still exist down here, deep inside our planet? The saurians who still remain with us, the lizards and crocodiles and alligators, up there in the rivers now so far above our heads, are feeble imitations of those great creatures of the past! I shudder when I think of meeting one of those original giants: thirty feet, perhaps, from nose to tail, and colossally strong.

No, no, I think to myself, there can no longer be such creatures, either on the face of the Earth or inside it . . .

And yet . . . can those toothmarks on the crowbar be made

by any living thing if it is not a crocodile ten times as huge as any that survive on the Earth's surface?

I find I am staring across this deep sea with wild and terrified eyes. Every moment, I expect some immense monster to rise from the depths!

How strange this light is, I continue to think. It is like being in the most enormous room imaginable, lit by a great lamp one cannot see!

For fear that the worst might happen, I pick up our weapons, one by one, making sure each is ready to be used. My uncle sees what I am doing, and nods. So he, too, fears the worst!

On the surface of the water there are bubblings, splashings, sometimes more than that. The water swells and then is sucked down again. Something must be moving below. It happens more and more often. The sea is more and more disturbed. We must be on our guard.

Tuesday, August 20. At last it is evening – the time of day when we feel a great need to sleep. Of course, in this continuing light there is no night, but we are very tired. Hans remains at the rudder, his eyes never closed. I don't know when he sleeps: but I find I am dozing, myself.

And then . . . an awful shock! The raft seems to have struck some hidden rock. It is lifted right out of the water, and even seems to be thrown some distance. "Eh!" cries my uncle. "What's happening?" And Hans raises his hand and points to where, about two hundred yards away, a great black mass is heaving. Then I know my worst fears have been realized.

"It's some . . . monster!" I cry.

"Yes," cries the Professor, "and over there is a huge sea lizard!"

"And beyond it . . . a crocodile! But who ever saw such a crocodile! Such hideous jaws! Such terrible teeth!"

"And a whale!" the Professor shouts. "See those enormous fins! And see how it blows air and water!"

And indeed two columns of water rise from the surface of the sea as he speaks, reaching an immense height before they fall back into the sea with an enormous crash. The whole cave in which this great sea is set, its walls and roof invisible to us, echoes with the sound of it. We are at the centre of the most tremendous uproar! And then we see – and how tiny we feel! – that we are in the middle of a great circle of these creatures. Here, a turtle, forty feet wide: here, a serpent even longer, its ghastly head peering out of the water. Wherever we look, there are more of them: great teeth, frightful eyes, great coiling bodies! They are everywhere! I snatch up my rifle, and think at once how useless it is. What effect would a bullet have on the armour that encases the bodies of these monsters?

There seems no hope for us. Though, suddenly, most of the creatures have plunged under the surface and are no longer to be seen, they leave behind a mighty crocodile and a prodigious sea serpent: and they are making towards us, and the end seems near. I think that, useless though it is, I will fire a shot. But Hans makes a sign for me to wait. For these monsters, having come so close to the raft, suddenly turn and make a rush at each other. In their fury they appear not to have seen us. And at that moment we realize how very small we are. To their great eyes, we must seem nothing bigger than an inch or so of floating scrap.

And so, in a thunder of broken water, the battle begins. At first I think all the other creatures have come to the surface and are taking part. *There* is a whale! – *there* a lizard! – a turtle! – and other monsters for which I can find no name. I point them out to Hans. But he shakes his head.

"*Tva!*" he cries.

"*Tva?* Two? Why does he say two? There are more than two!" I cry.

"No, Hans is right," says my uncle. "One of those monsters has the snout of a porpoise, the head of a lizard, the teeth of a crocodile . . . It is the ichthyosaurus, or great fish lizard."

"And the other?"

"The other is a serpent, but it has a turtle's shell. It is the plesiosaurus, or sea crocodile."

He is right! There seem to be half a dozen monsters, or more, but the truth is there are only two!

And ours are the first human eyes ever to look at these great primitive reptiles! I am amazed by the flaming red eyes of the ichthyosaurus, each bigger than a man's head. Those eyes, I know, are of enormous strength, since they have to resist the pressure of water at the very bottom of the ocean. The creature is a hundred feet long, at least, and when I see his tail rise out of the water, angrily flicked like the hugest whip you could imagine, I can guess at his width. His jaw is larger than

I'd ever dreamed a jaw could be, and I remembered that naturalists have said the jaw of the ichthyosaurus must have contained at least one hundred and eighty-two teeth. They were making their calculations, of course, from the fossilized bones of creatures they imagined had been extinct for millions of years. Now I, and Hans, and the Professor, are gazing, from our tiny raft, at a *living* ichthyosaurus, rising from an ocean deep inside the Earth!

The other creature is the mighty plesiosaurus, a serpent with a trunk like an immensely long cylinder, with a short thick tail and fins like the banks of oars in a Roman galley. Its body is enclosed in a shell, and its neck, flexible as a swan's, rises thirty feet above the surface of the sea.

No other human being has ever seen such a combat! They raise mountains of water, and time and again the raft seems about to be upset. Time and again we imagine we are drowned. The creatures hiss at each other – and the hissing is worse than the sound of the wildest winds you can imagine, all blowing together. Then they seize each other in a terrible grip, giant wrestlers: and then, break away again. And again comes the great hissing, the furious disturbance of the water!

And in the middle of it all, how tiny we are! We crouch on the raft, expecting that any moment it will be overturned and we shall drown in that wildly disturbed sea, hundreds of miles below the surface of the Earth: far, far from the sky, trees, the blessed fresh air!

And then, suddenly, ichthyosaurus and plesiosaurus disappear together under the waves. Their going down, in one enormous plunge, draws the sea down with them, as if a great hole had been made in the water, and we are nearly dragged down with them. For a while there is silence. The water grows calmer. And then, not far from the raft, an enormous shape appears. It is the head of the plesiosaurus.

The monster is mortally wounded. All we can make out is its neck, a serpent's. It is twisted and coiled in the agonies of death. With it the creature strikes the water as if with some great whip. Then it wriggles, as some vast worm might do, cut in two. Every dreadful movement stirs the sea violently, and we are nearly blinded as the tormented water sweeps over the raft. But bit by bit the great writhings die down, and at last the plesiosaurus lies dead on the surface.

As for the ichthyosaurus, he was surely recovering from the struggle in some deep cave. He could not have been unhurt. He must need to lick his wounds.

Or was he on his way to the surface again, to destroy us?

THE LAST MAN ALIVE

FROM *THE PURPLE CLOUD*

M. P. SHIEL

*The purple cloud is a poisonous vapour that brushes the
surface of the Earth and destroys all the human life on it.
Except, it seems, for one man, who during the time of the
cloud was exploring the Arctic, which the cloud did not touch.
He returns to England to find it as it was at the very
moment when the cloud had its fatal effect. This is in the
days of steam-trains: and he decides to make steam on any
engine he can find undamaged, and to head for London.*

I SAT AGAIN and rested, rose and roamed again, until after
six I found myself at another station named 'Priory'; and here
I saw two long trains, both bethronged, one on a siding, and
one at the up-platform.

On examining both engines, I found them of the old
steam-type, in one no water, but in that at the platform the
gauge showed some, and, on overhauling all the machinery, I
found it good, though rusted, with plenty of fuel, of oil, which
I supplemented from a shop near; and for ninety minutes my
mind and hands acted with an intelligence as it were
automatic, till I saw the fire blazing finely, the steam-gauge

registering; and when the safety-valve lever, whose load I lightened by two atmospheres, lifted, I jumped down to try to disconnect the string of carriages from the engine, but failed in this, the coupling being some automatism new to me; nor did I care. As it was now dark, and there was still some oil for bull's-eye and lantern, I lit them; then rolled driver and stoker, one to the platform, one upon the rails; and about 8.30 ran out from Dover, my throttle-valve pealing high a long falsetto through the bleak and desolate night.

My aim was London; but I knew nothing of the metals, their junctions, facing-points, sidings, shuntings, and complexities, nor was even sure whether I was raging towards, or away from, London; but just in proportion as my timorousness of the engine hardened into familiarity and self-confidence, I quickened speed, wilfully, with an obstinacy deaf and obdurate, till finally, from a crawl, I was flying at a shocking velocity, while something, tongue in cheek, seemed to whisper me, "there must be trains blocking the rails, at stations, in sheds, everywhere – it is a maniac's ride, a ride of death, Flying Dutchman's frenzy; remember your dark brigade of passengers who rock and bump together, and will suffer in a shock"; but stubbornly I thought, "they wished to go to London", and on I raged, not crazily exhilarated, I think, but feeling a wicked and morose unreason glow dully in my bosom, while I stoked begrimed at the fire-box, or caught sight of the corpse of horse or ox, of trees and fields receding, glooming homestead and farm, flowing ghostly past me.

Long, though, it did not last: I could not have been twenty

miles from Dover when, on a straight stretch of line, I made out before me a tarpaulined mass opposite a signal-box: and instantly callousness popped into panic in me. But even as I put on the brake, dragged at the link-gear lever, I understood that it was too late – rushed towards the gangway for a wild jump down an embankment to the right, but was flung forward by a series of rough bumps, caused by some ten oxen that lay there across the rails; and when I picked myself up and leapt, some seconds before the collision, the speed must have slackened, for I received no fracture, but lay in a semi-coma in a patch of yellow-flowering whin on level ground, just conscious of a conflagration on the rails forty yards away, and, all the dark hours, of vague thunder sounding from somewhere.

By five in the morning I was sitting up, rubbing my eyes, seeing in a dim light mixed with drizzle that the train of my last night's debauch was a huddled-up chaos of carriages and bodies, while on my right a five-barred gate swung with groans; and four yards from me a wee pony with a swollen wan belly, the picture of death; and dead wet birds . . .

I went following the rail-track on foot, the engines of both the trains in collision being smashed, knowing north from south by the sun, and, after many stoppages at houses, arrived, about eleven in the night, at a populous town.

By the Dane John and the Cathedral I recognized it as Canterbury, which I knew well, and walked up to the High Street, conscious for the first time of that regularly-repeated sound, like a sob or groan, which was proceeding from my throat. As there was no visible moon, and these old streets pretty dim, I had to pick my way, lest I should desecrate the dead with my foot, and they all should rise with hue-and-cry to hunt me. However, the bodies here were not numerous, most, as before, being foreigners: and these, scattered about this prim old city in that mourning darkness, presented such a spectacle of the baneful wrath of God, and all abomination of desolation, as broke me quite down at one place, where I stood constrained to jeremiads and sore sobbings and lamentations, crying out upon it all, God knows.

"Not numerous" – till I stood at the west entrance of the Cathedral, whence I could descry spreading up the darkling nave, to the lantern, to the choir, a phantasmagorical mass of forms, and, going a little inward, flashing three matches, peering nearer, I seemed to see the transepts, too, crowded, the south-west porch thronged, so that a great congregation must have flocked hither shortly before their doom overtook them . . .

Weary as I became, some morbid persistence sustained me, and I would not rest, so that four in the morning found me at a station afresh, industriously stooping, poor wretch, at the sooty task of getting another engine ready for travel, for nowhere hereabouts did I see any motorcars, all having fled westward; and this time when steam was up I succeeded in uncoupling the carriages from the engine, so by the time daylight glimmered I was gliding light away over the country, whither I did not know, but thinking of London.

Now I went with more wariness, and got on very well,

travelling seven days, seldom at night, never at more than twenty miles, slowing in tunnels. I do not know into what maze the train took me, for soon after leaving Canterbury it must have shunted down some branch-line, nor did the names of stations help me, for their situation relatively to London I seldom knew; and again and again was my progress interrupted by trains on my metals, when I would have to run back to some shunting or siding, and, in two instances, these being remotely behind, transhipped from my own to the impeding engine. On the first day I travelled unimpeded till noon, when I drove up in open country that seemed uninhabited for ages, only that half a mile off on a shaded sward was a house of artistic design, coated with tinted harling, the roof of red Ruabon tiles, with timbered gables, and I walked to it after another to-do with putting out the fire and laying a new one, the day lightsome and mild, with counties of white cloud lying quiet over the sky. I found in the house an outer and an inner hall, oil-paintings, a kind of museum, in a bedroom three women with servants'-caps and a footman arranged in a strange symmetrical way, head to head, like rays; and, as I stood looking at them, I could have sworn, my good God, that someone was coming up the stair – some creaking of the breeze in the house, increased a hundred-fold to my fevered hearing: for, used to this muteness of eternity that I have heard for years now, it is as though I hear sounds through an ear-trumpet. So I went down quick, and, after eating, and drinking some clary-water, made of brandy, sugar, cinnamon, and rose-water, which I found in plenty, I lay down on a sofa in the outer hall, and slept until midnight.

I went out then, still possessed with the greed to reach London, and, after getting the engine to rights, went off beneath sparkling black sky swarming with spawn of stars far-cast, some of them, I thought, not unlike this of mine, whelmed in an immensity of silence, with one life perhaps to see it, and hear its silence; and all the night I travelled, stopping twice only, once to get the coal from an engine which had blocked me, and once to drink some water, which I took care, as always, should be running water. When I felt my head nod about 4 a.m., I tossed myself, just outside the arch of a tunnel, upon a bank thick with stalks and flowers, the workings of early dawn being then in the east: and there, till near eleven, slept.

On waking, I noticed that the country now looked more like Surrey than Kent – that regular swelling of the land; but in fact, though it must have been either, it looked like neither, for already everything had an aspect of tending to a state of wild nature, and I could well divine that for a year at the least no hand had touched the land . . .

Two yards from the rails I saw when I stood up a rill at the foot of a rotten bit of fence, barely oozing itself onward under masses of stagnant fungoids; and here there was a sudden splash, and life, I catching sight of the hind legs diving of a frog; so, going to lie on my belly to pore over the wobbling little water, I presently saw three bleaks or ablets go gliding, tiny, low down among the moss-hair flying wild from the bottom-rocks, and I thought how gladly would I become one of them, with my home so thatched and shadowy, and my life drenched in their wide-eyed reverie. At all events, these little beings are living, the batrachians also, and, as I found the next day, chrysalides of one sort or another, for, to my profound emotion, I saw a little butterfly staggering in the air over the flower-garden of a rustic station named Butley.

It was while I was lying there, poring upon that brooklet, that a thought arose in me: for I said: "If now I be here alone, alone, alone . . . alone, alone . . . one on the earth . . . and my girth have a span of 25,000 miles . . . what will happen to my mind? Into what kind of creature shall I writhe and change? I may live two years so! What will have happened then? I may live five years – ten! What will have happened after the five? the ten? I may live twenty, fifty . . ."

How We Were Tracked by a Tripod

from *The White Mountains*

John Christopher

*The Earth has been conquered by beings from another planet,
who make human beings their slaves by capping them. When
he reaches the age of fifteen, a human has a metal cap driven
into his skull which enables his thoughts and feelings to be
controlled by the aliens. An English boy, Will, rebels against
this fate. He knows that other rebels have gathered in the
White Mountains: and he sets out on the dangerous journey
to join them. It takes him into what used to be France. After
he escapes from a Tripod, one of the enormously tall,
mechanical creatures who patrol the Earth on behalf of its
conquerors, Will joins up with Henry, who is English, and
Beanpole, who is French: heading for the White Mountains,
they find they are being closely pursued by a Tripod.*

THE MORNING WAS gloomy, matching our mood; the
pines were enshrouded in a thin grey cold mist, which brought
us to shivering wakefulness while there was still barely enough
light to see our way. We stumbled through the trees, trying to
warm ourselves by our activity, and gnawing on raw potatoes
as we went. We had not been able to see much of the valley

the night before, and could see nothing now. It grew more light, but visibility was limited by the mist. There was a circle of a few yards, and after that the trunks of trees melted into the surrounding monochrome.

Of course, we saw nothing of the Tripod. Nor did we hear anything: the only sound was the sound of our own progress and that, over the carpet of pine needles, was so quiet that it could not have carried much beyond the field of view, if as far. A day earlier, this would have been heartening, but we could not pretend that it made any difference that, for the present, our pursuer was out of sight and hearing. It had been so for well over twenty-four hours, and then had come, through the trackless forest of pines, to stand over us.

We came out of the pines into the wet grass which soaked our feet and the lower part of our legs. It was very cold. We had been setting a faster pace than usual, but the exercise had not warmed us. I was shivering, my teeth chattering a little. We did not talk much, and what we said was bare and unhopeful. There was no point in asking Beanpole if he had thought of a way out. One only had to look at his long miserable face, pinched by the cold, to see that he had not.

The valley bottomed out, and we bore to the west. The map had showed us that if we followed it for some miles we would find an easier ascent. We were continuing to go by the map automatically, for want of anything better. We heard the lonely gurgle and splash and chatter of water, and found a river and followed it. We had been travelling for some hours, and I was as chilled and wretched as at the start, and a good deal more hungry. There was no sign of food or life here.

Then, gradually, the mist lifted. The dirty grey turned whiter, became translucent, gleamed with silver, here and there admitted a shaft of brightness that dazzled briefly on the tumbling surface of the water before snuffing out. Our spirits lifted with it, to some extent, and when the sun appeared, first as a thin silver disc and at last as an orb of burning gold, we felt almost cheerful by comparison. I told myself that perhaps we had been wrong in thinking the Tripod had some magical way of tracking us. Perhaps its means of following us had been through senses – sight, hearing – which were only in degree better than our own. And if that were so, might not the long trek through the mist have lost us? It was not a rational optimism, but it made me feel better. The last of the mists trailed away into the distance, and we were traversing a broad sunlit valley, with the high ground on either side draped in white cloud. Birds were singing. Apart from them, we were entirely alone.

Until I heard a distant crackling far up on the hillside, and looked there and saw it, half-veiled in cloud but hideously real.

In the afternoon we found a clump of horse-radish, and pulled the roots up and ate them. The taste was bitter and fiery, but it was food. We had left the valley, starting a climb up long but fairly moderate slopes of rough scrubland, and the Tripod was out of view again. But not out of mind. The feeling of hopelessness, of being caught in a trap which in due course must close, continually strengthened. I had followed the fox hunts on foot back at Wherton, but I could have had no stomach for them after this. Even the sun, which beat down more warmly than ever out of a clear sky, could not cheer me. When, with its rays slanting low from the west, Beanpole called a halt, I dropped on to the grass, empty and exhausted. The other two, after resting a while, stirred themselves and began foraging, but I did not move. I lay on my back, eyes closed against the light, hands clasped under the back of my neck. I still did not move when they came back, arguing about whether one could eat snakes – Henry had seen one but failed to kill it – and whether, anyway, they were hungry enough to eat it raw since there was no kindling for a fire. I kept my eyes shut when Henry, in quite a different, sharper voice, said, "What's that?"

It would not, I was sure, be anything that mattered. Beanpole said something, in a lower voice, which I did not catch. They were whispering together. I kept my closed eyes on the sun, which would soon be gone behind the hills. They whispered again. Then Beanpole said, "Will."

"Yes."

"Your shirt is torn, under the arm."

I said, "I know. I ripped it on a thorn bush coming up from the river."

"Look at me, Will." I opened my eyes, and saw him standing over me, looking down. There was a strange look on his face. "What is it you have, under your arm?"

I got into a sitting position. "Under my arm? What are you talking about?"

"You do not know?" I had put my right hand under my left arm. "No, the other one."

I used my left arm this time, feeling into my arm-pit. I touched something whose texture was not the texture of flesh, but smoother and harder – something like a small metal button, on whose surface my finger tips traced faint corrugations, a kind of mesh. I craned my head round, trying to look at it, but could not. It seemed to melt into my skin, with no clear division between them. I looked up, and saw the other two watching me.

"What is it?"

"It is the metal of the Caps," Beanpole said. "It grows into the skin, as the Caps do."

"The Tripod . . ." I said. "When it caught me, outside the castle, do you think . . .?"

I did not need to finish the sentence. Their faces showed me what they thought. I said wildly, "You don't think I've been guiding it – that I'm under its control?"

Henry said, "It's been following since a few days after you caught up with us. We can't throw it off, can we? Have you got a better way of accounting for it?"

I stared at him. The mystery of the Tripod's ability to find us, time after time, and the mystery of the small metal button, somehow welded to my body – they could not be separated, they must belong together. And yet my mind was my own; I was no traitor. I had the same certainty of that as I had of my very existence. But how could I prove it? There was no way I could see.

Henry turned to Beanpole. "What are we going to do with him?"

Beanpole said, "We must think carefully, before we do anything."

"We haven't got time for that. We know he's one of them. He's been sending messages to it with his mind. He's probably sent one saying he's been found out. It may be coming after us right now."

"Will told us of the Tripod," Beanpole said. "That it caught him, and released him again – that he was unconscious and could remember nothing. If his mind had been a servant of the Tripods, would he have said those things? And would he not have taken care, when his shirt was torn, rather than lie so that we could see it? Moreover, it is very small, not like the Caps, and not near the brain."

"But it is tracking us through him!"

"Yes, I believe so. The compass – it points to the north, because there must be much iron there. If you bring other iron near, it will point to that. One cannot see or feel the thing that makes it do this. The Tripod caught him, going away from the castle, when everyone there was asleep. He was un-Capped, but it did not Cap him. Maybe it was curious about what he would do, where he was going. And put this thing on him which it could follow, like a needle on a compass."

It made sense: I was sure what he said was true. I could feel the button under my arm with every small movement I made – not hurting, but I knew it was there. Why had I not felt it before? The same thought must have occurred to Henry.

"But he must have known about it," he said. "A thing like that."

"Perhaps not. Do you have in your country . . . people who amuse, with animals, those who swing through the air from bars, strong men, and such?"

"The circus," Henry said. "I saw one once."

"There was one came to my town, with a man who did strange things. He told people to go to sleep, and to obey his commands, and they did as he ordered, even doing things which made them look foolish. Sometimes the commands lasted for a time. A sailor with a crippled hip walked with no limp for a week – afterwards, the pain and the limp returned."

"I can feel it now," I said.

"We have shown it to you," Beanpole said. "It may be that breaks the command."

Henry said impatiently, "None of this alters the facts. The Tripod can trace him through that thing, and can pick us up along with him."

I saw his point. I said, "There's only one thing to do."

"What is that?" Beanpole asked.

"If we separate, and I go a different way from you – it can follow me still, but you will be all right."

"A different way to the White Mountains? But you will still lead it there. Most likely, that is what it wishes."

I shook my head. "I won't go there. I'll double back."

"And be caught again. And Capped?"

. . . I hoped I was not going white with the fear I felt. I said: "It will have to catch me first."

"It will catch you," Beanpole said. "You have no chance of getting away."

I said, trying not to think of what it entailed, "I can head it away, at least."

There was a silence. It was, as I had said, the only thing to do, and they were bound to agree with it. There was no need, really, for them to say anything. I got to my feet, turning away from their faces. Beanpole said, "Wait."

"What for?"

"I said that we must think. I have been thinking. This thing under your arm – it is small, and though it is fastened to the skin I do not think it goes much beneath it."

He paused. Henry said, "Well?"

Beanpole looked at me. "It is clear of the big vein. But it will hurt if we cut it out."

I had not seen what he was driving at, and hope, when I did, made me dizzy.

"Do you think you can?"

"We can try."

I began stripping off my shirt. "Let's not waste any time on it!"

Beanpole was not to be hurried. He made me lie down, with my arm held up, and explored the button and the skin around it with his fingers. I wanted him to get on with it, but I was in his hands, and realized there was no point in showing my impatience. At last, he said, "Yes, it will hurt. I will do it as quickly as I can, but you will need something to bite on. And, Henry – you must hold his arm out, so that he cannot draw it back."

He gave me the leather strap of his pack to hold between my teeth; I felt the sour harsh taste of it on my tongue. The knife was one he had picked up in the great-city. It had a good edge, having been protected by a kind of grease, and he had spent some time sharpening it since then. It could not be too sharp for my liking. At a word from Beanpole, Henry took my arm, and stretched it out and back behind me. I was lying on my left hip, my face toward the ground. An ant scurried along and disappeared between blades of grass. Then there was the weight of Beanpole squatting over me, his left hand feeling again at the flesh under my arm, outlining the shape of the button. I was making a trial bite at the leather when he made the first cut, and my whole body jerked and I very nearly pulled my hand free from Henry's grasp. The pain was excruciating.

It was followed by another lance, and another. I tried to concentrate on the leather strap, through which my teeth seemed to be almost meeting. I was sweating so much that I felt drops of it rolling down the side of my face, and I saw one splash in the dust. I wanted to cry to him to stop, to let me have at any rate a rest from the pain, and was on the point of spitting the strap out to be able to speak when a new jab made me bite it again, and the side of my tongue with it. There was the hot salty taste of blood in my mouth, and tears in my eyes. Then, from a great distance, I heard him say: "You can let go now," and my hand and arm were free. The pain was furious still, but mild compared with what it had been a little earlier. Beanpole got up from me, and I started to drag myself to my feet. I had to move my arm to do so, and felt sick with what it did to me.

"As I thought," Beanpole said, "it is on the surface only. Observe."

I got rid of the gag, and looked at what he was holding in his hand. It was silvery grey, about half an inch in diameter, thicker in the centre and tapering towards the edge. It was solid, but gave the impression of hundreds of tiny wires just below the surface. Attached to it were the bloody scraps of my flesh which Beanpole had cut away.

Beanpole poked the button with his finger.

"It is curious," he said. "I would like to study this. It is a pity we must leave it."

His gaze was one of dispassionate interest. Henry, who was also looking, had a greenish tinge to his face. Staring at the gobbets of flesh adhering, nausea rose in me again, and this time I had to turn away to be sick. When I recovered, Beanpole was still looking at the button.

Gasping, I said: "Throw it away. And we'd better get going. The further we get away from here, the better."

He nodded reluctantly, and dropped it in the grass. He said to me, "Your arm – does it hurt much?"

"I wouldn't care to bowl fast for the next hour or two."

"Bowl fast?"

"In cricket. It's a game we play in our country. Oh, never mind. Let's get a move on. It will take my mind off it."

"There is a herb which heals wounds. I will look for it on the way."

A good deal of blood had flowed and was still flowing down my side. I had been mopping it up with my shirt, and I now rolled the shirt up into a ball, wadded it under my arm, and walked with it in that position. My hopeful suggestion that travelling would take my mind off the pain did not work out very well. It went on hurting just as much, if not more. But I was rid of the Tripod's button, and each jolting step left it further behind.

We were continuing to climb over rough, but mostly open country. The sun was setting on our right; on the other side our long shadows were almost abreast of us. We were not talking, in my case because I was too occupied with gritting my teeth. It was, if one were in the mood for appreciating it, a lovely and peaceful evening. Calm and still. No sound, except . . .

We stopped, and listened. My heart seemed to contract, and for a moment the pain was blotted out by the greater power of fear. It came from behind, faint but seeming to grow louder every instant: the hideous warbling ululation which we had heard in the cabin of the *Orion* – the hunting call of the Tripods.

Seconds later it was in sight, coming round the base of the hill and, unmistakably, climbing towards us. It was some miles away, but coming on fast – much faster, I thought, than its usual rate of progress.

Henry said, "The bushes . . ."

He did not need to say any more; we were all three running. What he had indicated offered one of the few bits of cover on the hillside, the only one within reasonable reach. It was a small thicket of bushes, growing to about shoulder height. We flung ourselves in amongst them, burrowed into the centre, and crouched down there.

I said, "It can't still be after me. Can it?"

"The button," Beanpole said. "It must be that cutting it out gave an alarm. So it has come after you, and this time hunting."

"Did it see us, do you think?" Henry asked.

"I do not know. It was far away, and the light is poor."

In fact, the sun had gone down; the sky above our hiding place was drained of gold, a darker blue. But still terrifyingly clear – much lighter than it had been the morning I had left the castle. I tried to console myself with the thought that I had been much nearer to it, also. The howling was louder and closer. It must have reached and passed the place where Beanpole had conducted the operation on me. Which meant . . .

I felt the ground shiver under me, and again and again with still greater force. Then one of the Tripod's legs plunged across the blue, and I saw the hemisphere, black against the arc of sky, and tried to dig myself down into the earth. At that moment the howling stopped. In the silence I heard a different, whistling sound of something whipping terribly fast through the air and, glancing fearfully, saw two or three bushes uprooted and tossed away.

Beside me, Beanpole said, "It has us. It knows we are here. It can pull the bushes out till we are plainly seen."

"Or kill us, pulling them out," Henry said. "If that thing hit you . . ."

I said: "If I showed myself . . ."

"No use. It knows there are three."

"We could run different ways," Henry said. "One of us might get away."

I saw more bushes sail through the air, like confetti. You do not get used to fear, I thought; it grips you as firmly every time. Beanpole said:

"We can fight it."

He said it with a lunatic calm, which made me want to groan. Henry said:

"What with? Our fists?"

"The metal eggs." He had his pack open already, and was rummaging in it. The Tripod's tentacle whistled down again. It was ripping the bushes up systematically. A few more passes – half a dozen at most – would bring it to us. "Perhaps these were what our ancestors used, to fight the Tripods. Perhaps that is why they were in the underground Shmand-Fair – they went out from there to fight them."

I said: "And they lost! How do you think . . .?"

He had got the eggs out. He said, "What else is there?"

Henry said, "I threw mine away. They were too much trouble to carry."

The tentacle sliced into the bushes, and this time we were scattered with earth as it pulled them up. Beanpole said:

"There are four." He handed one each to Henry and me. "I will take the others. If we pull out the rings, count three, then stand up and throw. At the leg that is nearest. The hemisphere is too high."

This time I saw the tentacle *through* the bushes as it scooped up more. Beanpole said, "Now!"

He pulled the rings from his eggs, and Henry did the same. I had taken mine in my left hand, and I needed to transfer it to the right. As I did so, pain ripped my armpit again, and I dropped it. I was fumbling on the ground to pick it up when Beanpole said, "Now!" again. They scrambled to their feet, and I grabbed the last egg, ignoring the pain of the movement, and got up with them. I ripped out the ring just as they threw.

The nearest foot of the Tripod was planted on the slope, thirty yards or so above us. Beanpole's first throw was wild – he did not get within ten yards of his target. But his second throw, and Henry's, were close to the mark. One of them hit metal, with a clang that we could hear. Almost at once they exploded. There were three nearly simultaneous bangs, and fountains of earth and dust sprouted into the air.

But they did not obscure one plain fact: the eggs had done no damage to the Tripod. It stood as firmly as before, and the tentacle was swishing down, this time directly towards us. We started to run, or rather, in my case, prepared to. Because before I could move, it had me round the waist.

I plucked at it with my left hand, but it was like trying to bend a rock. It held me with amazing precision, tight but not crushing, and lifted me as I might lift a mouse. Except that a mouse could bite, and I could do nothing against the hard gleaming surface that held me. I was lifted up, up. The ground shrank below me, and with it the figures of Beanpole and Henry. I saw them darting away like ants. I was steeple-high, higher. I looked up, and saw the hole in the side of the hemisphere. And remembered the iron egg still clutched in my right hand.

How long was it since I had pulled the ring out? I had forgotten to count in my fear and confusion. Several seconds – it could not be long before it exploded. The tentacle was swinging me inwards now. The hole was forty feet away, thirty-five, thirty. I braced myself back, straining against the encircling band. Pain leapt in my arm again, but I ignored it. I hurled the egg with all my strength, and what accuracy I could muster. I thought at first that I had missed, but the egg hit the edge of the opening and ricocheted inside. The tentacle continued to carry me forwards. Twenty feet, fifteen, ten . . .

Although I was nearer, the explosion was not as loud as the others had been, probably because it happened inside the hemisphere. There was just a dull, rather hollow bang. Despair came back: that was my last chance gone. But at that instant I felt the metal holding me relax and fall away.

I was three times the height of a tall pine; my bones would smash against the ground when I landed. I clutched desperately at the thing against which, a few seconds earlier, I had been struggling. My hands gripped the metal, but I was falling, falling. I looked at the ground, and closed my eyes as it rushed up to meet me. And then there was a jerk which almost tore me from my hold, and the falling stopped. My feet shivered, a few inches from the surface. All I had to do was let go, and step down.

The others came to me. We stared up, in awe, at the Tripod. It stood there, seemingly unharmed. But we knew it was finished, destroyed, lifeless.

THE WAR OF THE WORLDS

AN EXTRACT

H.G. WELLS

It was sometime about 1890, and nobody in England
expected trouble – especially trouble from another planet.
So that few knew what to think when . . . things apparently
landed at spots near London, coming apparently from space,
and caused craters: and when it was seen that, inside those
craters . . . machines were being assembled. Slowly, bit by bit,
people did realize that something was weirdly and horribly
wrong. Things were coming out of the craters, and people were
being killed; and in the end, some began to run for it, and
then more and more – leaving their homes, puzzled and very
frightened. It was from Mars that these dangerous visitors
appeared to have arrived: and now they were moving across
the country, huge, armoured, using . . . Heat-Rays.
The storyteller was at Weybridge, on the River Thames.

WE REMAINED AT Weybridge until midday, and at that hour we found ourselves at the place near Shepperton Lock where the Wey and Thames join. Part of the time we spent helping two old women to pack a little cart. The Wey has a treble mouth, and at this point boats are to be hired, and there was a ferry across the river. On the Shepperton side was an inn, with a lawn, and beyond that the tower of Shepperton Church – it has been replaced by a spire – rose above the trees.

Here we found an excited and noisy crowd of fugitives. As yet the flight had not grown to a panic, but there were already far more people than all the boats going to and fro could enable to cross. People came panting along under heavy burdens; one husband and wife were even carrying a small outhouse door between them, with some of their household goods piled thereon. One man told us he meant to try to get away from Shepperton Station.

There was a lot of shouting, and one man was even jesting. The idea people seemed to have here was that the Martians were simply formidable human beings, who might attack and sack the town, to be certainly destroyed in the end. Every now and then people would glance nervously across the Wey, at the meadows towards Chertsey, but everything over there was still.

Across the Thames, except just where the boats landed, everything was quiet, in vivid contrast with the Surrey side. The people who landed there from the boats were tramping off down the lane. The big ferry-boat had just made a journey. Three or four soldiers stood on the lawn of the inn, staring and jesting at the fugitives, without offering to help. The inn was closed, as it was now within prohibited hours.

"What's that!" cried a boatman, and "Shut up, you fool!" said a man near me to a yelping dog. Then the sound came again, this time from the direction of Chertsey, a muffled thud – the sound of a gun.

The fighting was beginning. Almost immediately unseen batteries across the river to our right, unseen because of the trees, took up the chorus, firing heavily one after the other. A woman screamed. Everyone stood arrested by the sudden stir of battle, near us and yet invisible to us. Nothing was to be seen save flat meadows, cows feeding unconcernedly for the most part, and silvery pollard willows motionless in the warm sunlight.

"The sojers 'll stop 'em," said a woman beside me doubtfully. A haziness rose over the tree-tops.

Then suddenly we saw a rush of smoke far away up the river, a puff of smoke that jerked up into the air, and hung, and forthwith the ground heaved underfoot and a heavy explosion shook the air, smashing two or three windows in the houses near, and leaving us astonished.

"Here they are!" shouted a man in a blue jersey. "Yonder! D'yer see them? Yonder!"

Quickly, one after the other, one, two, three, four of the armoured Martians appeared, far away over the little trees, across the flat meadows that stretch towards Chertsey, and striding hurriedly towards the river. Little cowled figures they seemed at first, going with a rolling motion and as fast as flying birds.

Then, advancing obliquely towards us, came a fifth. Their armoured bodies glittered in the sun, as they swept swiftly forward upon the guns, growing rapidly larger as they drew nearer. One on the extreme left, the remotest, that is, flourished a huge case high in the air, and the ghostly terrible

Heat-Ray I had already seen on Friday night smote towards Chertsey, and struck the town.

At the sight of these strange, swift, and terrible creatures, the crowd along the water's edge seemed to me to be for a moment horror-struck. There was no screaming or shouting, but a silence. Then a hoarse murmur and a movement of feet – splashing from the river. A man, too frightened to drop the portmanteau he carried on his shoulder, swung round and sent me staggering with a blow from the corner of his burden. A woman thrust at me with her hand and rushed past me. I turned, too, with the rush of the people, but I was not too terrified for thought. The terrible Heat-Ray was in my mind. To get under water! That was it!

"Get under water!" I shouted unheeded.

I faced about again, and rushed towards the approaching Martian – rushed right down the gravelly beach and headlong into the water. Others did the same. A boatload of people putting back came leaping out as I rushed past. The stones under my feet were muddy and slippery, and the river was so low that I ran perhaps twenty feet scarcely waist-deep. Then, as the Martian towered overhead scarcely a couple of hundred yards away, I flung myself forward under the surface. The splashes of the people in the boats leaping into the river sounded like thunderclaps in my ears. People were landing hastily on both sides of the river.

But the Martian machine took no more notice for the moment of the people running this way and that than a man would of the confusion of ants in a nest against which his foot had kicked. When, half suffocated, I raised my head above water the Martian's hood pointed at the batteries that were still firing across the river, and as it advanced it swung loose what must have been the generator of the Heat-Ray.

In another moment it was on the bank, and in a stride wading half-way across. The knees of its foremost legs bent at the farther bank, and in another moment it had raised itself to its full height again, close to the village of Shepperton. Forthwith the six guns, which, unknown to anyone on the right bank, had been hidden behind the outskirts of that village, fired simultaneously. The sudden near concussions, the last close upon the first, made my heart jump. The monster was already raising the case generating the Heat-Ray, as the first shell burst six yards above the hood.

I gave a cry of astonishment. I saw and thought nothing of the other four Martian monsters: my attention was riveted upon the nearer incident. Simultaneously two other shells burst in the air near the body as the hood twisted round in time to receive, but not in time to dodge, the fourth shell.

The shell burst clean in the face of the thing. The hood bulged, flashed, was whirled off in a dozen tattered fragments of glittering metal.

"Hit!" shouted I, with something between a scream and a cheer.

I heard answering shouts from the people in the water about me. I could have leapt out of the water with that momentary exultation.

The decapitated colossus reeled like a drunken giant; but it did not fall over. It recovered its balance by a miracle, and, no longer heeding its steps, and with the camera that fired the Heat-Ray now rigidly upheld, it reeled swiftly upon Shepperton. The living intelligence, the Martian within the hood, was slain and splashed to the four windows of heaven, and the thing was now but a mere intricate device of metal whirling to destruction. It drove along in a straight line, incapable of guidance. It struck the tower of Shepperton Church, smashing it down as the impact of a battering-ram might have done, swerved aside, blundered on, and collapsed with a tremendous impact into the river out of my sight.

A violent explosion shook the air, and a spout of water, steam, mud, and shattered metal, shot far up into the sky. As the camera of the Heat-Ray hit the water, the latter had incontinently flashed into steam. In another moment a huge wave, like a muddy tidal bore, but almost scaldingly hot, came sweeping round the bend up-stream. I saw people struggling shorewards, and heard their screaming and shouting faintly above the seething and roar of the Martian's collapse.

For the moment I heeded nothing of the heat, forgot the patent need of self-preservation. I splashed through the tumultuous water, pushing aside a man in black to do so, until I could see round the bend. Half a dozen deserted boats pitched aimlessly upon the confusion of the waves. The fallen Martian came into sight down-stream, lying across the river, and for the most part submerged.

Thick clouds of steam were pouring off the wreckage, and through the tumultuously whirling wisps I could see, intermittently and vaguely, the gigantic limbs churning the water and flinging a splash and spray of mud and froth into the air. The tentacles swayed and struck like living arms, and, save for the helpless purposelessness of these movements, it was as if some wounded thing struggled for life amidst the waves. Enormous quantities of a ruddy brown fluid were spurting up in noisy jets out of the machine.

My attention was diverted from this sight by a furious yelling, like that of the thing called a siren in our manufacturing towns. A man, knee-deep near the towing-path, shouted inaudibly to me and pointed. Looking back, I saw the other Martians advancing with gigantic strides down the river-bank from the direction of Chertsey. The Shepperton guns spoke this time unavailingly.

At that I ducked at once under water, and, holding my breath until movement was an agony, blundered painfully along under the surface as long as I could. The water was in a tumult about me, and rapidly growing hotter.

When for a moment I raised my head to take breath, and throw the hair and water from my eyes, the steam was rising in a whirling white fog that at first hid the Martians altogether. The noise was deafening. Then I saw them dimly, colossal figures of grey, magnified by the mist. They had passed by me, and two were stooping over the frothing tumultuous ruins of their comrade.

The third and fourth stood beside him in the water, one perhaps two hundred yards from me, the other towards Laleham. The generators of the Heat-Rays waved high, and the hissing beams smote down this way and that.

The air was full of sound, a deafening and confusing conflict of noises, the clangorous din of the Martians, the crash of falling houses, the thud of trees, fences, sheds, flashing into flame, and the crackling and roaring of the fire. Dense black smoke was leaping up to mingle with the steam from the river, and as the Heat-Ray went to and fro over Weybridge, its impact was marked by flashes of incandescent white, that gave place at once to a smoky dance of lurid flames. The nearer houses still stood intact, awaiting their fate, shadowy, faint and pallid in the steam, with the fire behind them going to and fro.

For a moment, perhaps, I stood there, breast-high in the almost boiling water, dumbfounded at my position, hopeless of escape. Through the reek I could see the people who had been with me in the river scrambling out of the water through the reeds, like little frogs hurrying through grass from the advance of a man, or running to and fro in utter dismay on the towing-path.

Then suddenly the white flashes of the Heat-Ray came leaping towards me. The houses caved in as they dissolved at its touch, and darted out flames; the trees changed to fire with a roar. It flickered up and down the towing-path, licking off the people who ran this way and that, and came down to the water's edge not fifty yards from where I stood. It swept across the river to Shepperton, and the water in its track rose in a boiling wheal crested with steam. I turned shoreward.

In another moment the huge wave, well-nigh at the boiling point, had rushed upon me. I screamed aloud, and scalded, half-blinded, agonized, I staggered through the leaping, hissing water towards the shore. Had my foot stumbled, it would have been the end. I fell helplessly, in full sight of the Martians, upon the broad, bare gravelly spit that runs down to mark the angle of the Wey and Thames. I expected nothing but death.

I have a dim memory of the foot of a Martian coming down within a score of yards of my head, driving straight into the loose gravel, whirling it this way and that, and lifting again; of a long suspense, and then of the four carrying the débris of their comrade between them, now clear, and then presently faint, through a veil of smoke, receding interminably, as it seemed to me, across a vast space of river and meadow. And then, very slowly, I realized that by a miracle I had escaped.

Homecoming

Stephen David

AT THE BEGINNING and end of the typhoon season, when the winds were rising and falling, you could use the current to glide between the Cities in a flitter with its small motor turned off. The favoured game was to ignore the flight decks and glide straight in at one of the portals, swooping over the galleries and terrifying the people walking there. Naturally, this was extremely dangerous. If you missed the portal, the impact with the City's hull could kill you; if it didn't, the two-kilometre drop to the ground probably would. It was a very popular game, and though it wasn't illegal to turn your motor off, it was very illegal to fly in populated areas of the Cities.

Jann had never played the Game. The idea of hurtling through the air with nothing between him and the ground was terrifying. He sometimes had nightmares of falling, hurtling down, seeing the twin Cities towering above him, then turning over in the air to see the ground and the waving heads of the tall fever trees spinning crazily beneath him. Each time, he would wake, sometimes shouting.

It was just such a dream that woke him one night. It was the middle of the season of Roaring Winds and as he lay, sweating, in his bunk, he could feel the swaying motion as the City strained against its massive mooring cables. In the bunk below him his sister Katya stirred and mumbled. Jann threw back his quilt, slipped to the ground and padded quietly into the tiny kitchen. His father was sitting quietly at the counter, watching a scientific programme on the small viewing screen. He looked up.

"Can't sleep?"

"I had the dream again," Jann said. He climbed on the stool next to his father's and sat, rubbing his eyes.

"The falling dream?" Jann nodded. This was the fifth time since the typhoons had started.

"Well," his father said, "you'd better stay up till the dream's gone. Look." He pointed at the viewing screen. "They're showing the lift-off simulations." On the screen a computer image showed the City slowly revolving. Down the side of the screen a scale showed that from base to top the City was just over two kilometres high. Narrow at the base, it broadened out to the kilometre-deep cylinder that housed the living and industrial areas, then tapered again towards the top where the command centres were. Coloured arrows showed the wind direction. At first the arrows moved slowly, then gradually got faster. The City was spinning, like a top, the speed of rotation increasing as the thrust motors augmented the wind's effect. Again, the speed increased, and again, until the lines of the City were a blur. Then it was moving forwards and upwards, its rotation forcing it out to break free of the planet's weak gravity. Instead of sailing majestically a kilometre or so above the surface, harvesting the fever trees where they could, the Cities would finally break free entirely and sail where those who had built them had intended them to go: into space, into the galaxy – and home. The long exile would be over.

"When will we go?" Jann asked.

"Next typhoon season," his father said. "We need another half-year's good harvesting, then we'll have supplies to last us years in space."

Jann frowned. "Tomas didn't want us to go."

"I think Tomas was just repeating what his parents said."

"No," said Jann, irritated. "He thought a lot about it. He said we'd been here hundreds of years and no one on Earth would remember us, and even if we got back there we wouldn't be happy. He said we should just build small ships and send a few people back to make contact. There must be lots of inhabited planets by now, and we wouldn't have to go all the way back to Earth before finding one."

"No," said his father, with an air that Jann knew meant the discussion was over, "there would be no point. This planet will never be a good place to live. We don't want to spend our lives trapped in these floating Cities – and even if *I* have to, there's no reason for you to. In my lifetime or yours we've got to go Home, back where we belong. And it's a long journey. On a small ship, the crew might be dead of old age before they got anywhere."

"Well," said Jann, "Tomas is staying."

"Tomas is dead, Jann," his father said softly. "He played the Game and he fell. No one could survive that."

"No," said Jann. "I suppose not." He slid off the stool and went back to his bunk and a dreamless sleep.

The typhoon roared on. From the Cities to the horizon little could be seen through the clouds of reddish pollen blown by the shrieking gales. The preparations for the Return continued. In the great public halls people listened to lectures on why they were going, talks on Earth's history and culture. In the long corridors, the shopping plazas, and the cafés, they wondered: how long would it take, would any of them live to see the Homecoming? Might they roam space for decades, for hundreds of years, wandering the galaxy lost and hopeless? And if they found Earth, what would it be like? Would they be remembered – the descendants of the colonists who had disappeared hundreds of years before? Might Earth even be a dead planet, devastated by war or epidemic? On and on went the talk, round and round in circles. And in the tiny living quarters, families listened to the instructions blaring from the City's public address system and practised strapping themselves into their bunks as they would have to when the time of departure came.

Slowly the winds dropped. The quiet season came and the harvesting went on. People continued to talk. Every evening Jann would listen to his parents discussing the departure. He thought about Tomas, his friend, who would not be going.

There came a day when the winds began to rise again. Standing in the vast gallery that overlooked the space beween his City, City One, and City Two, Jann could see the first flitters swoop through the early pollen clouds, wheeling and circling before dropping towards the flight decks or portals of the City. That was the way Tomas had gone. No one had seen it happen, but he had left City One and was never seen again. His name was added to the list of victims of the Game; his family and friends mourned him; and Jann wondered. He wondered, because when it happened he had not been surprised. While some of Tomas's friends argued about whether he had smashed into the City's hull or lost control and plummeted to his death, Jann thought of the conversation he and Tomas had had only a few days before Tomas disappeared.

They had been walking along the main corridor on 'D' level, on their way home from class. As so often, they were talking about departure. At times like these, Jann always felt that Tomas might be right: he was so passionate, but also so logical. It was only when he repeated Tomas's arguments to his parents that they seemed not to work so well.

"*We'll* be foreigners," Tomas had said. "We've all grown up in the Cities, we only know Earth from the material in the libraries – and all of that was recorded hundreds of years ago . . ."

"But we *came* from Earth," Jann protested. "They must remember that a shipfull of colonists went missing. Maybe they've even been searching –" Tomas laughed, though not pleasantly.

"When someone goes down in the Game," he said harshly, "how long do they look for them?" He did not wait for an answer. "These days, they don't. They assume the person's death. And they'd only have to search a few square miles to make sure, not half an interstellar space. C'mon, Jann: a ship travelling at near light speeds goes missing after passing through an asteroid belt? Who's gonna search? You assume the whole thing's dust and carry on looking for the next inhabitable planet. Shall I tell you what will happen if we turn up near a human-occupied planet?" Jann grunted, unwilling, but Tomas steamed on. "Two massive ships – *they* won't know they're cities – appear in your segment of space, so big you could fit an Earth-type city into each of them. If we're *lucky*, they surround us and escort us out of their bit of the galaxy. If we're unlucky, they just blast us out of the space. We don't *belong* there – we belong *here*." He gestured round. Although it looked as if he was pointing at the wide, crowded corridor, it seemed to Jann that he meant something else.

"But this planet is so hostile –" Jann began to say.

"It's not the planet," said Tomas fiercely, "it's *us*! We never tried. When the colony ship landed here, they took one look at the place, said 'Ugh!' and started planning ways of escaping. And ever since, every effort we're capable of, all our energy, have been put towards getting away. If we'd spent all that time and cleverness in figuring out ways of staying we wouldn't be cooped up in these rusty tin cans now . . ." Jann looked around. True, parts of the City were looking a little dilapidated. The Council always said there was no time for 'minor maintenance'.

"But Tomas," Jann said, feeling as ever slow and witless in the face of Tomas's conviction, "everyone else seems to agree we've got to go. Surely people wouldn't go on believing something that's not true for so long?"

"*Every*one? No, not everyone. I'll tell you who doesn't agree: the harvesters don't agree. And those of us who play the Game don't agree. Now, why should that be?" The harvesters were those who used the flitters for their real purpose − gathering the pulpy fruit of the vast fever trees, which the Cities converted into almost every kind of eating and drinking material. Jann shook his head, and Tomas went on, "Because we're the ones who go outside and look at the planet. The harvesters get right down to the surface, almost, and we at least smell the air and feel the wind on our faces. Jann, this planet is *beautiful*!"

"How can you say that? Half the year is typhoon season. The rest of the year it's just barren except for the fever trees."

"Come and glide, Jann. Come tomorrow. Then you'll understand."

Jann shook his head. Then he said, "Be careful, Tomas. We've only one season left before we depart. Don't end up smashed to bits down there."

Tomas gave him a curious smile. "I won't," he said, "but I'm not going. And I'm not the only one."

"But how −" Before Jann could say any more, Tomas broke away.

"If you want to know, come and play the Game tomorrow. Otherwise − well, if I happen not to be around anymore, don't worry too much . . ." Abruptly, he was gone. A few days later Jann heard that he had disappeared, was assumed dead.

He missed Tomas. Although they frequently argued, Jann felt that this left them both stronger. Tomas was unorthodox, a dreamer. Jann seemed cautious, conservative – often, it was his quiet practicality that punctured Tomas's wilder balloons such as his scheme to smuggle a flitter, piece by piece, to the very top of the City (where there was almost no atmosphere) and ride it down all the way to the flight decks. But Jann did not like Tomas's challenges. Without him – and he had few other friends – he felt half-empty. And it had been a whole season now.

It had happened gradually. First, he took to watching the flitters in the Game. Then, he began to sneak out at dawn to watch the dusty red sunrise. Even then a few daring youngsters would be playing the Game.

After several mornings, Jann found himself heading, as if propelled by some force outside himself, down to the flight deck. It was a large, rectangular hangar, open to the sky at one end. Down one wall stood a row of flitters, down the other a row of large hoppers, used to carry the fever tree pulp up to the Cities. A group of youngsters was standing by a flitter at the open end of the hangar; beyond the portal the flight deck jutted out, a narrow platform hanging over the void. As Jann slowly approached the group, a black-painted flitter swooped noiselessly down. Its skis slid smoothly on the flight deck, the flitter's wings folding back as it swept into the hangar. It came to a halt by the waiting group. The hood slid back and a girl stepped out. About Jann's age, she had long black hair and a fierce-looking face. He recognized her as a girl from City Two called Keri. Tomas had spoken admiringly of her. There was a burst of applause from the group. Then one of them, a boy Jann didn't know, broke away and took Keri's place in the flitter. The motor hummed into life, and within seconds the flitter was speeding down the flight deck. As soon as it was clear, its motor would be switched off.

Keri ignored the group and set off down the hangar. As she neared Jann he stepped in front of her, blocking her way. She stopped.

"Tomas said you'd come in the end," she said.

"What did he mean?"

"About what?"

"About staying here. And not being the only one."

"Why don't you ask him?"

"How can I?" Jann was fast getting furious. "He's dead!"

"If you really think that," she said slowly and emphatically, gazing for the first time into his eyes, "*Why are you here?*" Furiously, he grabbed her arm, but she pulled away and set off down the hangar. He followed her.

"Every question I ask, you ask me one back. I'm his friend. *Where is he?*"

She did not break her stride. "Are your family going?" she asked.

He was bewildered. "Going? Of course. Everyone is."

"Tomas isn't."

"But he's −" A terrible thought struck Jann for the first time. "You mean he's alive . . . down there, on the surface?" She didn't answer. "But if he is then they ought to send a rescue party, get him back. He'll *die*. Maybe he's hurt. And the fever trees . . . he'll get the fever . . ." His voice had risen and he was suddenly aware that he was shrieking.

At last she stopped. "All right," she said, "have you been to see Tomas's parents?" Shamefaced, Jann admitted he had not. "Fine," Keri said, "then we'll go to see them. You can tell them what you think." Helplessly, he trailed in her wake.

Jann was shocked when Keri did not bother to press the buzzer of the apartment, more shocked when she coolly pressed the code combination to let them in, and astounded when they found the place empty. There was nothing to show that Tomas or his parents had ever been there. None of the little personal possessions that people used to differentiate the otherwise identical living quarters. It was incomprehensible. If the family were dead, the quarters would be occupied by new people by now – the public dormitories were hugely overcrowded and there were long waiting lists for the private apartments. That this apartment was empty could only mean that no one knew the family were gone. Except Keri. And himself. Abruptly he sat on the floor, leant back against a bare wall.

"Where are they?" Keri stood in the middle of the room, arms folded, looking down at him, a faint smile on her face.

"With Tomas," she said.

"Are they hiding?"

"In a way."

"In City Two?"

"There's only one way to find out, Jann. Play the Game.

198

That's what Tomas told you, wasn't it?"

"But if he's in Two, there's no need — we can just go over on the ferry."

"Jann, it's a matter of *trust*." Keri knelt down, her voice low. "Tomas wanted you to come out with us, he wanted to tell you . . . what was happening. But you wouldn't come, so he wasn't allowed to say anything. He still wants to talk to you, but you've got to give something in return. You've got to make the trip. Then he'll tell you everything."

Jann knew well enough how to do it. He'd spent many hours in the huge freefall chambers at the top of the City, piloting a flitter in the artificial winds, secure in the knowledge that if anything went wrong an automatic safety device would immediately land machine and pilot softly and safely. This, though, would not be recreation. He thought of his dream. Keri was watching him closely.

"If you don't," she said, "you'll never see Tomas again." Weakly he nodded, feeling sick and afraid.

Somehow, when they got back to the hangar, the portal at the far end seemed menacing, and Jann fancied he could see the unpredictable winds gusting past. He thought of the emptiness below the flight deck and shuddered. Keri pointed him towards a flitter.

"I'll keep beside you," she said. "Mostly, once we're out there we open the hoods. The air's thin but breathable. You don't have to, but I'd recommend it. What you *do* have to do is switch the motor off."

He slipped into the cockpit, slid the hood shut and started

the motor. He did everything quickly because he was scared and did not want to think. As the flitter slid gently along the hangar towards the flight deck he realized he'd forgotten to let the wings swing shut. He pressed the button. He was dimly aware of Keri's flitter to his right. Then they were out of the hangar and on the flight deck and he gasped. All around him was light, bright and shadowy, dappled with clouds of moisture and pollen. In the distance City Two revolved slowly, magnificently, its hull plates sparkling in the light. Suddenly Jann realized the flitter was in the air, had left the flight deck. Forgetting to be afraid he cut the motor. And opened the hood.

The air was warm. There was a smell, something Jann couldn't identify: somehow it make him feel hungry, it was rich and appetizing but like nothing he had smelled in the City. And the colours: from a rich indigo above him, so blue and deep he felt he could lose himself in it, to a pale translucent blue in the distance ahead of him. He looked over to Keri's flitter and, suddenly joyous, waved. He saw her grin, then she waved her hand and pointed downwards. The nose of her flitter dipped. Suddenly alarmed, Jann kept his flitter on an even course, constantly adjusting as the winds gusted around him. He lost sight of Keri and wondered where she had gone. Ahead he could see City Two's flight deck, now only a matter of minutes away. It hadn't been so bad. He would talk to Tomas then get the ferry back.

Above and to his left there was an angry buzzing. Startled he looked up and there, hovering dangerously close – *and with its motor on* – was Keri's flitter. His brain screamed at him to evade her, but before his hands could obey, she had dropped to her right. Her wing hit his and, with a lurch, his flitter dropped. Frantically Jann fought to get the little craft back on an even keel. After what seemed hours, it levelled off. Sweating, he looked round. No sign of Keri, and he still had the height to make it to the flight deck. And now he knew. Whatever was going on, he had been told too much. Keri had tried to kill him.

She attacked again, just as his finger was poised over the button to start the motor. Again the wings met and Jann's craft lurched sickeningly downwards. Again, he fought to regain control, not daring to start the motor until he was flying level. And then he had it, the nose straightened, and he pressed it again. Nothing. And he was now too low to make the flight deck.

Keri appeared at his right again. He glared at her. To his astonishment she smiled and made an unmistakable 'follow me' sign. Swiftly, he considered the alternatives. Keri banked steeply to the right and began a long, slow spiral down. Mentally shrugging, Jann followed.

His flitter passed within metres of City Two. This far down there were no observation posts, just ventilation ducts, sluices, inspection hatches. Above, he could see the vast outlets of the thrust motors, the hull beneath them blackened. Then he was below the City looking up. He felt dizzy at the sight of two kilometres of towering metal looming over him. He began to feel that it was about to fall on top of him, and hastily looked down. For the first time in his life, Jann saw a landscape without a city floating above it. He was now only a thousand metres up and could see below him a large patch of fever trees. Beyond them was a flat expanse of something that glinted, from which a silver ribbon wound across the flat, reddish landscape. There was no sound except for the rush of wind. Spiralling below him, he could see Keri's flitter.

Only a minute later they were below the level of the fever trees, whose odd, bulbous shapes strangely echoed the shapes of the Cities that floated above them. Below the bulbous plants sprouted the sharp leaves, metres across, that gave the trees their name.

Between the plants and the strange, glinting area, was an expanse of flat ground and it was here that Keri landed. Jann brought his flitter in behind her. As he did so, his pleasure in the glide down evaporated in a burst of anger at what she had done. As soon as his flitter had halted he leapt from the cockpit and ran furiously towards her. Keri, standing by her flitter, kept her ground and, as he approached, pointed behind him. Something in her face stopped him, and he turned. There, standing at the edge of the grove of fever trees, was Tomas, and his parents.

It was quiet and peaceful in the shade of the trees. The leaves rose for some metres, leaving enough space beneath them for the small settlement of huts constructed from the fibre of the trees. In the foliage above small creatures chittered comfortably, clicking their tongues in a dozy, muttering way. Beyond the edge of the grove, past the two flitters, water lapped gently on the stony shore, reflecting the starlight. There was a soft murmur of voices as people talked after the evening meal. Jann was sitting with Keri, and with Tomas and his parents outside their hut.

"I told you," Tomas said, but this time there was no anger in his voice, "we're not going. This is our home." He pointed at the lake. "Until today, you had no idea that lakes even existed. Let me tell you: swimming in water is as much fun as flitting. *And* you can drink it. *And* there are fish there to eat." They had just eaten fish. Jann had never tasted anything so wonderful. He was bemused – not at what he was seeing, but that so few people in the Cities understood.

"I thought it was all hostile," he said, "and the leaves of the plants, and the pollen – people *died*."

"At first," said Tomas's father. "People who touched the leaves got fever and died after terrible hallucinations. But we soon became resistant: it's been hundreds of years since a death. But people weren't willing to try. They'd left Earth in a colony ship because Earth was so overcrowded it was choking to death. They were full of dreams, obsessed with finding a fresh planet, one where clear streams ran through green meadows and high mountains sparkled against a clear blue sky. But one ship, carrying a thousand colonists, had an accident. An asteroid damaged it so badly it lost contact with the others and had to seek refuge on the nearest planet." He paused. "Here. And what did they find? Lots of stony ground and the fever trees. Within days there were deaths. They stayed in the ship, trying to repair it – and failed. They were stuck on a planet that was the opposite of all they had hoped for."

The groups of people around the huts had fallen silent, listening now. They must all know the story, Jann thought, but they need to hear it again.

"It was hard at first, just surviving. But in the ship they had all they needed to make the most of any planet they were on. They had mining equipment, laboratories, computerized factories, flitters, you name it. The one thing they didn't have was the capacity to build a new fusion plant to get them off the planet.

"Now, the idea was that when they landed, they'd build a town and start making the planet a good place to live. But what our ancestors did instead was to bed down in the disabled colony ship and start figuring out ways to get away.

"They'd only been here a month or so when the typhoon season started. They weren't ready for it, so that halved the population. But when it was all over, one of them remembered something he'd seen . . ." Tomas's father paused dramatically and gestured upwards. "As the winds built up the fever trees began spinning. And just when the typhoon started they spun so hard they took off into the sky, flinging pollen every which way."

"So there *is* a reason why the shapes look the same," Jann exclaimed.

"It's the same principle. The planet's got low gravity and that typhoon can act like a whip on a spinning top. Mind you, it took hundreds of years. The first cities were top heavy. They crashed. It was only about four generations ago that One and

Two finally became habitable. And in all those hundreds of years, we learned so little about this planet. Oh, we learned to harvest the pulp from the trees. But then we got into the Cities and most of us turned our backs on the outside world. Most people up there aren't capable even of thinking that living down here is possible. And in a few days . . ."

"They'll leave without you," Jann broke in. Around him, the family smiled. Tomas gestured at the group of huts, the people sitting quietly in their doorways in the warm air, the soft murmur of conversation.

"Yes," he said quietly, "but they're leaving us in our home. Jann, people have been slipping away from the Cities for some time now. We aren't the only settlement. We know this planet isn't Paradise: but there *is* enough to eat and we *will* survive and, in the end, we will cultivate it and build towns and, one day, even cities."

"But even if we fail," said Keri, "at least we'll do it here, not wandering the galaxy trying to get back to the very thing we fled from."

"Jann, stay with us," said Tomas. Jann looked around him. Starlight softly illuminated the quiet clearing. Above them, the giant fever trees swayed. Warm air carried the smell of the water that sparkled beyond the trees. He sighed.

The next morning Jann climbed into the flitter. Keri had repaired her sabotage of the motor. He settled in the seat and looked down at Tomas and Keri.

"I've got to go," he said. "All my life I've lived with the dream of all of us going back into space and finding the rest of the human race. There must be lots of planets by now with people on them. We seem so – cut off here. Nothing's happened here, ever."

"Jann," said Tomas gently, "that's because the people who wanted to leave wouldn't *let* anything happen."

"Well," said Jann, "yes, but I must go. I like your world, but I must go."

"And I thought *I* was the dreamer," said Tomas.

Jann laughed. "I'll come back," he said, "and by then there'll be a nice big town here, and you'll be mayor."

"He won't," said Keri, "I will."

The little flitter climbed up, over the fever trees and towards the great Cities poised in the sky. City One loomed closer and closer. Deftly, Jann piloted the flitter onto the flight deck and taxied into the hangar. He was home.

Below, Tomas and Keri gazed up. The waves on the lake were getting higher, whipped up by the gathering winds. Dust was blowing and pollen from the trees filled the air. There was a creaking noise from the great trunks of the fever trees.

Above them, the two shining cities began to revolve more quickly.

All Summer in a Day

Ray Bradbury

"READY?"

"Ready."

"Now?"

"Soon!"

"Do the scientists really know? Will it happen today, will it?"

"Look, look; see for yourself!"

The children pressed to each other like so many roses, so many weeds, intermixed, peering out for a look at the hidden sun.

It rained.

It had been raining for seven years; thousands upon thousands of days compounded and filled from one end to the other with rain, with the drum and gush of water, with the sweet crystal fall of showers and the concussion of storms so heavy they were tidal waves come over the islands. A thousand forests had been crushed under the rain and grown up a thousand times to be crushed again. And this was the way life was forever on the planet Venus, and this was the schoolroom of the children of the rocket men and women who had come to a raining world to set up civilization and live out their lives.

"It's stopping, it's stopping!"

"Yes, yes!"

Margot stood apart from them, from these children who could never remember a time when there wasn't rain and rain and rain. They were all nine years old, and if there had been a day, seven years ago, when the sun came out for an hour and showed its face to the stunned world, they could not recall. Sometimes, at night, she heard them stir, in remembrance, and she knew they were dreaming and remembering gold or a yellow crayon or a coin large enough to buy the world with. She knew that they thought they remembered a warmness, like a blushing in the face, in the body, in the arms and legs and trembling hands. But then they always awoke to the tatting drum, the endless shaking down of clear bead necklaces upon the roof, the walk, the gardens, the forest, and their dreams were gone.

All day yesterday they had read in class, about the sun. About how like a lemon it was, and how hot. And they had written small stories or essays or poems about it:

I think the sun is a flower,

That blooms for just one hour.

That was Margot's poem, read in a quiet voice in the still classroom while the rain was falling outside.

"Aw, you didn't write that!" protested one of the boys.

"I did," said Margot. "I *did*."

"William!" said the teacher.

But that was yesterday. Now, the rain was slackening, and

the children were crushed to the great thick windows.

"Where's teacher?"

"She'll be back."

"She'd better hurry, we'll miss it!"

They turned on themselves, like a feverish wheel, all tumbling spokes.

Margot stood alone. She was a very frail girl who looked as if she had been lost in the rain for years and the rain had washed out the blue from her eyes and the red from her mouth and the yellow from her hair. She was an old photograph dusted from an album, whitened away, and if she spoke at all her voice would be a ghost. Now she stood, separate, staring at the rain and the loud wet world beyond the huge glass.

"What're *you* looking at?" said William.

Margot said nothing.

"Speak when you're spoken to." He gave her a shove. But she did not move; rather, she let herself be moved only by him and nothing else.

They edged away from her, they would not look at her. She felt them go away. And this was because she would play no games with them in the echoing tunnels of the underground city. If they tagged her and ran, she stood blinking after them and did not follow. When the class sang songs about happiness and life and games, her lips barely moved. Only when they sang about the sun and the summer did her lips move, as she watched the drenched windows.

And then, of course, the biggest crime of all was that she

had come here only five years ago from Earth, and she remembered the sun and the way the sun was and the sky was, when she was four, in Ohio. And they, they had been on Venus all their lives, and they had been only two years old when the last sun came out, and had long since forgotten the colour and heat of it and the way that it really was. But Margot remembered.

"It's like a penny," she said, once, eyes closed.

"No it's not!" the children cried.

"It's like a fire," she said, "in the stove."

"You're lying, you don't remember!" cried the children.

But she remembered and stood quietly apart from all of them, and watched the patterning windows. And once, a month ago, she had refused to shower in the school shower rooms, had clutched her hands to her ears and over her head, screaming the water mustn't touch her head. So after that, dimly, dimly, she sensed it, she was different and they knew her difference and kept away.

There was talk that her father and mother were taking her back to Earth next year; it seemed vital to her that they do so, though it would mean the loss of thousands of dollars to her family. And so, the children hated her for all these reasons, of big and little consequence. They hated her pale snow face, her waiting silence, her thinness and her possible future.

"Get away!" The boy gave her another push. "What're you waiting for?"

Then for the first time, she turned and looked at him. And what she was waiting for was in her eyes.

"Well, don't wait around here!" cried the boy, savagely. "You won't see nothing!"

Her lips moved.

"Nothing!" he cried. "It was all a joke, wasn't it?" He turned to the other children. "Nothing's happening today. *Is* it?"

They all blinked at him and then, understanding, laughed and shook their heads. "Nothing, nothing!"

"Oh, but," Margot whispered, her eyes helpless. "But, this is the day, the scientists predict, they say, they *know*, the sun . . ."

"All a joke!" said the boy, and seized her roughly. "Hey, everyone, let's put her in a closet before teacher comes!"

"No," said Margot, falling back.

They surged about her, caught her up and bore her, protesting, and then pleading, and then crying, back into a tunnel, a room, a closet, where they slammed and locked the door. They stood looking at the door and saw it tremble from her beating and throwing herself against it. They heard her muffled cries. Then, smiling, they turned and went out and back down the tunnel, just as the teacher arrived.

"Ready, children?" She glanced at her watch.

"Yes!" said everyone.

"Are we all here?"

"Yes!"

The rain slackened still more.

They crowded to the huge door.

The rain stopped.

It was as if, in the midst of a film concerning an avalanche, a tornado, a hurricane, a volcanic eruption, something had, first, gone wrong with the sound apparatus, thus muffling and finally cutting off all noise, all of the blasts and repercussions and thunders, and then, secondly, ripped the film from the projector and inserted in its place a peaceful tropical slide which did not move or tremor. The world ground to a standstill. The silence was so immense and unbelievable that you felt your ears had been stuffed or you had lost your hearing altogether. The children put their hands to their ears. They stood apart. The door slid back and the smell of the silent, waiting world came in to them.

The sun came out.

It was the colour of flaming bronze and it was very large. And the sky around it was a blazing blue tile colour. And the jungle burned with sunlight as the children, released from their spell, rushed out, yelling, into the summertime.

"Now, don't go too far," called the teacher after them. "You've only one hour, you know. You wouldn't want to get caught out!"

But they were running and turning their faces up to the sky and feeling the sun on their cheeks like a warm iron; they were taking off their jackets and letting the sun burn their arms.

"Oh, it's better than the sunlamps, isn't it?"

"Much, much better!"

They stopped running and stood in the great jungle that covered Venus, that grew and never stopped growing, tumultuously, even as you watched it. It was a nest of octupuses, clustering up great arms of flesh-like weed, wavering, flowering in this brief spring. It was the colour of rubber and ash, this jungle from the many years without sun. It was the colour of stones and white cheeses and ink.

The children lay out, laughing, on the jungle mattress, and heard it sigh and squeak under them, resilient and alive. They ran among the trees, they slipped and fell, they pushed each other, they played hide-and-seek and tag but most of all they squinted at the sun until tears ran down their faces, they put their hands up at that yellowness and that amazing blueness and they breathed of the fresh fresh air and listened and listened to the silence which suspended them in a blessed sea of no sound and no motion. They looked at everything and savoured everything. Then, wildly, like animals escaped from their caves, they ran and ran in shouting circles. They ran for an hour and did not stop running.

And then –

In the midst of their running, one of the girls wailed.

Everyone stopped.

The girl, standing in the open, held out her hand.

"Oh, look, look," she said trembling.

They came slowly to look at her opened palm.

In the centre of it, cupped and huge, was a single raindrop. She began to cry, looking at it.

They glanced quickly at the sky.

"Oh. Oh."

A few cold drops fell on their noses and their cheeks and their mouths. The sun faded behind a stir of mist. A wind blew cool around them. They turned and started to walk back towards their underground house, their hands at their sides, their smiles vanishing away.

A boom of thunder startled them and like leaves before a new hurricane, they tumbled upon each other and ran. Lightning struck ten miles away, five miles away, a mile, a half-mile. The sky darkened into midnight in a flash.

They stood in the doorway of the underground house for a moment until it was raining hard. Then they closed the door and heard the gigantic sound of the rain falling in tons and avalanches everywhere and forever.

"Will it be seven more years?"

"Yes, seven."

Then one of them gave a little cry.

"Margot!"

"What?"

"She's still in the closet where we locked her."

"Margot."

They stood as if someone had driven them, like so many stakes, into the floor. They looked at each other and then looked away. They glanced out at the world that was raining now and raining and raining steadily. They could not meet each other's glances. Their faces were solemn and pale. They looked at their hands and feet, their faces down.

"Margot."

One of the girls said, "Well . . .?"

No one moved.

"Go on," whispered the girl.

They walked slowly down the hall in the sound of cold rain. They turned through the doorway to the room, in the sound of the storm and thunder, lightning on their faces, blue and terrible. They walked over to the closet door slowly and stood by it.

Behind the closet door was only silence.

They unlocked the door, even more slowly, and let Margot out.

GRENVILLE'S PLANET

MICHAEL SHAARA

WISHER DID NOT see the brightness because he was back aft alone. In the still ship he sat quietly, relaxed. He was not bored. It was just that he had no interest. After fourteen years in the Mapping Command even the strangest of the new worlds was routine to him and what little imagination he had was beginning to centre upon a small farm he had seen on the southern plains of Vega VII.

The brightness that Wisher did not see grew with the passing moments. A pale young man named Grenville, who was Wisher's crewman, watched it for a long while absently. When the gleam took on brilliance and a blue-white, dazzling blaze Grenville was startled. He stared at the screen for a long moment, then carefully checked the distance. Still a few light minutes away, the planet was already uncommonly bright.

Pleasantly excited, Grenville watched the planet grow. Slowly the moons came out. Four winked on and ringed the bright world like pearls in a vast necklace. Grenville gazed in awe. The blueness and the brightness flowed in together; it was the most beautiful thing that Grenville had ever seen.

Excited, he buzzed for Wisher. Wisher did not come.

Grenville took the ship in close and now it occurred to him to wonder. The glare was incredible. That a planet should shine like that, an enormous facet of polished glass, was incredible. Now, as he watched, the light began to form vaguely into the folds of clouds. The blue grew richer and deeper. Long before he hit the first cloud layer, Grenville knew what it was. He pounded the buzzer. Wisher finally came.

When he saw the water in the screen he stopped in his tracks.

"Well I'll be damned!" he breathed.

Except for a few scuds of clouds it was blue. The entire world was blue. There was the white of the clouds and the icecaps, but the rest was all blue and the rest was water.

Grenville began to grin. A world of *water*!

"Now, how's *that* for a freak?" he chuckled. "One in a million, right, Sam? I bet you never saw anything like that."

Wisher shook his head, still staring. Then he moved quickly to the controls and set out to make a check. They circled the planet with the slow, spiralling motion of the Mapping Command, bouncing radar off the dark side. When they came back into the daylight they were sure. There was no land on the planet.

Grenville, as usual, began to chatter.

"Well, naturally," he said, "it was bound to happen sooner or later. Considering Earth, which has a land area covering only one fourth . . . ."

"Yep," nodded Wisher.

". . . and when you consider the odds, chances are that there are quite a number of planets with scarcely any land area at all."

Wisher had moved back to the screen.

"Let's go down," he said.

Grenville, startled, stared at him.

"Where?"

"Down low. I want to see what's living in that ocean."

Because each new world was a wholly *new* world and because experience therefore meant nothing, Wisher had decided a long while ago to follow the regs without question. For without the regs, the Mapping Command was a death trap. Nowhere in space was the need for rules so great as out on the frontier where there were no rules at all. The regs were complex, efficient and all-embracing; it was to the regs that the men of Mapping Command owed their lives and the rest of Mankind owed the conquest of space.

But inevitably, unalterably, there were things which the regs could not have foreseen. And Wisher knew that too, but he did not think about it.

According to plan, then, they dropped down into the stratosphere, went further down below the main cloud region and levelled off at a thousand feet. Below them, mile after rolling, billowy mile, the sea flowed out to the great bare circle of the horizon.

With the screen at full magnification, they probed the water.

It was surprising, in all that expanse of sea, to observe so little. No schools of fish of any kind, no floating masses of seaweed, nothing but a small fleet shape here and there and an occasional group of tiny plant organisms.

Wisher dropped only a hundred or so feet lower. In a world where evolution had been confined underwater it would be best to keep at a distance. On the other worlds to which he had come Wisher had seen some vast and incredible things. *Eight hundred feet up*, he thought, *is a good safe distance.*

It was from that height, then, that they saw the island.

It was small, too small to be seen from a distance, was barely five miles in length and less than two miles wide. A little brown cigar it was, sitting alone in the varying green-blue wash of the ocean.

Grenville began to grin. Abruptly he laughed out loud. Grenville was not the kind of man who is easily awed, and the sight of that one bare speck, that single stubby persistent butt of rock alone in a world of water, was infinitely comical to him.

"Wait'll we show the boys *this,*" he chuckled to Wisher. "Break out the camera. My God, what a picture *this* will make!"

Grenville was filled with pride. This planet, after all, was *his* assignment. It was his to report on, his discovery – he gasped. They might even name it after *him*.

He flushed, his heart beat rapidly. It had happened before. There were a number of odd planets named after men in the Mapping Command. When the tourists came they would be coming to Grenville's Planet, one of the most spectacular wonders of the Universe.

While the young man was thus rejoicing, Wisher had brought the ship around and was swinging slowly in over the island. It was covered with some kind of brownish-green, stringy vegetation. Wisher was tempted to go down and check for animal life, but decided to see first if there were any more islands.

Still at a height of eight hundred feet, they spiralled the planet. They did not see the second island, radar picked it out for them.

This one was bigger than the first and there was another island quite near to the south. Both were narrow and elongated in the cigar-like shape of the first, were perhaps twenty miles in length and were encrusted with the same brown-green vegetation. They were small enough to have been hidden from sight during the first check by a few scattered clouds.

The discovery of them was anticlimactic and disappointing. Grenville would have been happier if there was no land at all. But he regained some of his earlier enthusiasm when he remembered that the tourists would still come and that now at least they would be able to land.

There was nothing at all on the night side. Coming back out into the daylight, Wisher cautiously decided to land.

"Peculiar," said Wisher, peering at the dunes of the beach.

"What is?" Grenville eyed him through the fish-bowls of their helmets.

"I don't know." Wisher turned slowly, gazed around at the shaggy, weedy vegetation. "It doesn't feel right."

Grenville fell silent. There was nothing on the islands that could hurt them, they were quite sure of that. The check had revealed the presence of a great number of small, four-footed animals, but only one type was larger than a dog, and that one was slow and noisy.

"Have to be careful about snakes," Wisher said absently, recalling the regs on snakes and insects. Funny thing, that. There were very few insects.

Both men were standing in close to the ship. It was the rule, of course. You never left the ship until you were absolutely sure. Wisher, for some vague reason he could not define, was not sure.

"How's the air check?"

Grenville was just then reading the meters. After a moment he said, "Good."

Wisher relaxed, threw open his helmet and breathed in deeply. The clean fresh air flowed into him, exhilarating. He unscrewed his helmet entirely, looking around.

The ship had come down on the up end of the beach, a good distance from the sea, and was standing now in a soft, reddish sand. It was bordered on the north by the open sea and to the south was the scrawny growth they had seen from above. It was not a jungle – the plants were too straight and stiff for that – and the height of the tallest was less than ten feet. But it was the very straightness of the things, the eerie regularity of them which grated in Wisher's mind.

But, breathing in the cool sea air of the island, Wisher began to feel more confident. They had their rifles, they had the ship and the alarm system. There was nothing here that could harm them.

Grenville brought out some folding chairs from the ship. They sat and chatted pleasantly until the twilight came.

Just before twilight two of the moons came out.

"Moons," said Wisher suddenly.

"What?"

"I was just thinking," Wisher explained.

"What about the moons?"

"I wasn't thinking exactly about them, I was thinking about the tide. Four good-sized moons in conjunction could raise one heck of a tide."

Grenville settled back, closing his eyes.

"So?"

"So that's probably where the land went."

Grenville was too busy dreaming about his fame as discoverer of Grenville's Planet to be concerned with tides and moons.

"Let the techs worry about that," he said without interest.

The tide could very well be the cause. When the four moons got together and started to pull they would raise a tremendous mass of water, a grinding power that would slice away the continent edges like no erosive force in history. Given a billion years in which to work – but Wisher suddenly remembered a peculiar thing about the island.

If the tides had planed down the continent of this planet, then these islands had no right being here, certainly not as sand and loose rock. Just one tide like the ones those moons could raise would be enough to cut the islands completely away. Well maybe, he thought, the tides are very far apart, centuries even.

He glanced apprehensively at the sky. The two moons visible were reassuringly far apart.

He turned from the moons to gaze at the sea. And then he remembered the first thought he had had about this planet – that uncomfortable feeling that the first sight of land had dispelled. He thought of it now again.

Evolution.

A billion years beneath the sea, with no land to take the first developing mammals. What was going on, right now as he watched, beneath the placid rolling surface of the sea?

It was a disturbing thought. When they went back to the ship for the night Wisher did not need the regs to tell him to seal the airlock and set the alarm screens.

The alarm that came in the middle of the night and nearly scared Wisher to death turned out to be only an animal. It was one of the large ones, a weird bristling thing with a lean and powerful body. It got away before they were up to see it, but it left its photographic image.

In spite of himself, Wisher had trouble getting back to sleep, and in the morning he was silently in favour of leaving for the one last star they would map before returning to base. But the regs called for life specimens to be brought back from all livable worlds whenever possible, whenever there was no 'slight manifestation of danger'. Well, here it was certainly possible. They would have to stay long enough to take a quick sampling of plants and animals and of marine life too.

Grenville was just as anxious to get back as Wisher was, but for different reasons. Grenville, figured Grenville, was now a famous man.

Early in the morning, then, they lifted the ship and once more spiralled the planet. Once the mapping radar had recorded the size and shape and location of the islands, they went in low again and made a complete check for life forms.

They found, as before, very little. There were the bristling things, and – as Wisher had suspected – a great quantity of snakes and lizards. There were very few observable fish. There were no birds.

When they were done they returned to the original island. Grenville, by this time, had a name for it. Since there was another island near it, lying to the south, Grenville called that one South Grenville. The first was, of course, North Grenville. Grenville chuckled over that for a long while.

"Don't go too near the water."

"All right, mama," Grenville chirped, grinning. "I'll work the edge of the vegetation."

"Leave the rifle, take the pistol. It's handier."

Grenville nodded and left, dragging the specimen sack. Wisher, muttering, turned towards the water.

It is unnatural, he thought, *for a vast warm ocean to be so empty of life. Because the ocean, really, is where life begins.* He had visions in his mind of any number of vicious, incredible, slimy things that were alive and native to that sea and who were responsible for the unnatural sterility of the water. When he approached the waves he was very cautious.

The first thing he noticed, with a shock, was that there were no shellfish.

Not any. Not crabs or snails or even the tiniest of sea beings. Nothing. The beach was a bare, dead plot of sand.

He stood a few yards from the waves, motionless. He was almost positive, now, that there was danger here. The shores of every warm sea he had ever seen, from Earth on out to Deneb, had been absolutely choked with life and the remnants of life. There were always shells and fish scales, and snails, worms, insects; bits of jellyfish, tentacles, minutiae of a hundred million kinds, cluttering and crowding every square inch of the beach and sea. And yet here, now, there was nothing. Just sand and water.

It took a great deal of courage for Wisher to approach those waves, although the water here was shallow. He took a quick water sample and hurried back to the ship.

Minutes later he was perched in the shadow of her side, staring out brooding over the ocean. The water was Earth-water as far as his instruments could tell. There was nothing wrong with it. But there was nothing much living in it.

When Grenville came back with the floral specimens Wisher quietly mentioned the lack of shellfish.

"Well, hell," said Grenville, scratching his head painfully, "maybe they just don't like it here."

And maybe they've got reason, Wisher said to himself. But aloud he said, "The computer has finished constructing the orbits of those moons."

"So?"

"So the moons conjunct every 112 years. They raise a tide of six hundred feet."

Grenville did not follow.

"The tide," said Wisher, smiling queerly, "is at least four hundred feet higher than any of the islands."

While Grenville stared, still puzzled, Wisher grunted and kicked at the sand.

"Now where the hell do you suppose the animals came from?"

"They should be drowned," said Grenville slowly.

"Right. And would be, unless they're amphibian, which they're not. Or unless a new batch evolves every hundred years."

"Um." Grenville sat down to think about it.

"Don't make sense." he said after a while.

Having thoroughly confounded Grenville, Wisher turned away and paced slowly in the sand. *The sand*, he thought distractedly, *that's another thing. Why in heck is this island here at all?*

Artificial.

The word popped unbidden into his brain.

That would be it. That would have to be it.

The island was artificial, was − restored. Put here by whoever or whatever lived under the sea.

Grenville was ready to go. He stood nervously eyeing the waves, his fingers clamped tightly on the pistol at his belt, waiting for Wisher to give the word.

Wisher leaned against the spaceship, conveniently near the airlock. He regretted disturbing Grenville.

"We can't leave yet," he said calmly. "We haven't any proof. And besides, there hasn't been any 'manifestation of danger'."

"We have proof enough for me," Grenville said quickly.

Wisher nodded absently.

"It's easy to understand. Evolution kept right on going, adapting and changing just as it does everywhere else in the Universe. Only here, when the mammals began coming up on to the land, they had no room to expand. And they were all being washed away every hundred years, as the tides rose and fell and the continents wore down below tide level.

"But evolution never stopped. It continued beneath the sea. Eventually it came up with an intelligent race.

"God knows what they are, or how far they've progressed. They must be pretty highly-evolved, or they couldn't have done something like this" – he broke off, realizing that the building of the islands was no clue. The ancient Egyptians on Earth had built the pyramids, certainly a much harder job. There was no way of telling how far evolved this race was. Or what the island was for.

Zoo?

No. He shook that out of the confusion of his mind. If the things in the sea wanted a zoo they would naturally build it below the surface of the water, where they themselves could travel with ease and where the animals could be kept in airtight compartments. And if this was a zoo, then by now there should have been visitors.

That was one more perplexing thing. Why had nothing come? It was unbelievable that an island like this should be left completely alone, that nothing had noticed the coming of their ship.

And here his thoughts broke again. They would not be just fish, these things. They would need . . . hands. Or tentacles. He pictured something like a genius squid, and the hair on his body stiffened.

He turned back to Grenville.

"Did you get the animal specimens?"

Grenville shook his head. "No. Just plants. And a small lizard."

Wisher's face, lined with the inbred caution of many years, now at last betrayed his agitation. "We'll have to get one of those things that set off the alarm last night. But to heck with the rest. We'll let HQ worry about that." He stepped quickly into the airlock, dragging the bag of specimens. "I'll pack up," he said; "you go get that thing."

Grenville turned automatically and struck off down the beach.

He never came back.

At the end of the third hour after Grenville had gone, Wisher went to the arms locker and pulled out a heavy rifle. He cursed the fact that he had no small scout sled. He could not take the ship. She was too big and unwieldy for low, slow flying and he could not risk cracking her up.

He was breaking the regs, of course. Since Grenville had not come back he must be considered dead and it was up to

Wisher to leave alone. A special force would come back for Grenville, or for what was left of him. Wisher knew all that. He thought about it while he was loading the rifle. He thought about the vow he had made never to break the regs and he went right on loading the rifle. He told himself that he would take no chances and if he didn't find Grenville right away he would come back and leave, but he knew all along that he was breaking the regs. At the same time he knew that there was nothing else to do. This was the one reg he had never faced before and it was the one reg he would always break. For Grenville or for anyone else. For a skinny young fool like Grenville, or for anyone else.

Before he left he took the routine precautions concerning the ship. He set the alarm screens to blast anything that moved within two hundred feet of her. If Grenville came back before him it would be all right because the alarm was set to deactivate when it registered the sound pattern of either his or Grenville's voice. If Grenville came back and didn't see him, he would know that the alarm was on.

And if no one came back at all, the ship would blow by itself.

The beach was wide and curved on out of sight. Grenville's deep heel prints were easy to follow.

Stiffly, in the wind, the stalks of the brown vegetation scratched and rustled. Wisher walked along Grenville's track. He wanted to call, but stopped himself. No noise. He must make no noise.

This is the end of it, he kept saying to himself. When I get out of this I will go home.

The heel prints turned abruptly into the alien forest. Wisher walked some distance farther on, to a relatively clear space. He turned, stepping carefully, started to circle the spot where Grenville had gone in. The wood around him was soggy, sterile. He saw nothing move. But a sharp, shattering blast came suddenly to him in the still air.

The explosion blossomed and Wisher jerked spasmodically. The ship. Something was at the ship. He fought down a horrible impulse to run, stood quiet, gun poised, knowing that the ship could take care of itself. And then he stepped slowly forward. And fell.

He fell through a soft light mat of bushes into a hole. There was a crunching snap and he felt metal rip into his legs, tearing and cracking the bones. He went up to his shoulders. He knew in a flash, with a blast of glacial fear, what it was. *Animal trap*.

He reached for his rifle. But the rifle was beyond him. A foot past his hand, it lay on the floor of the wood near him. His legs, his legs . . . he felt the awful pain as he tried to move.

It blazed through his mind and woke him. Out of his belt he dragged his pistol, and in a sea of pain, held upright by the trap, he waited. He was not afraid. He had broken the regs, and this had happened, and he had expected it. He waited.

Nothing came.

Why? Why?

This had happened to Grenville, he knew. Why?

It had happened to him now, and for a moment he could

not understand why he did not seem to care, but was just . . . curious. Then he looked down into the hole and saw the hot redness of his own blood, and as he watched it bubble he realized that he was dying.

He had very little time. He was hopeful. Maybe something would come and at least he would see what they were. He wanted awfully for something to come. In the red mist which was his mind he debated with himself whether or not to shoot it if it came, and over and over he asked himself why, why? Before something came, unfortunately, he died.

The traps had been dug in the night. From out the sea they had come to dig in the preserve – for a preserve was what the island was, was all that it could have been – and then returned to the sea to wait.

For the ship had been seen from the very beginning, and its purpose understood. The best brains of the sea had gathered and planned, the enormous, manta-like people whose name was unpronounceable but whose technology was not far behind Earth's, met in consultation and immediately understood. It was necessary to capture the ship. Therefore the Earthmen must be separated from it, and it was for this reason that Wisher had died.

But now, to the astonishment of the things, the ship was still alive. It stood silent and alone in the whiteness of the beach, ticking and sparkling within itself, and near it, on the bloodied sand, were the remains of the one that had come too close. The others had fled in terror.

Time was of no importance to the clever, squid-like beings.

They had won already, could wait and consider. Thus the day grew late and became afternoon, and the waves – the aseptic, sterile waves which were proof in themselves of the greatest of all oceanic civilizations – crumbled whitely on the beach. The things exulted. The conquest of space was in their hands.

Within the ship, of course, there was ticking, and a small red hand moved towards zero.

In a little while the ship would blow, and with it would go the island, and a great chunk of the sea. But the beings could not know. It was an alien fact they faced and an alien fact was unknowable. Just as Wisher could not have known the nature of the planet, these things could not now foresee the nature of the ship and the wheel had come full circle. Second by second, with the utter, mechanical loyalty of the machine, the small red hand crept onward.

The waves near the beach were frothy and white.

A crowd was forming.

THE FEAR SHOUTER

JAY WILLIAMS

THE ISS CADETS' lounge was generally not the sort of cosy nook in which to do some quiet thinking, but today it sounded like a recording of twenty football crowds rolled into one and played backwards. It had begun with a relatively simple argument between C3 Loesser and C2 Geoghan, but by degrees everybody in and out of earshot had been drawn into it, and when you get half a hundred lively Space Service officers-in-training between the ages of 15 and 18 trying to out-talk each other, you have a place unsuitable for bringing a maiden aunt to tea.

In the centre of this tohu-bohu, Loesser, her hair plastered damply over her forehead, was still doggedly saying, "All right. You claim an alien race that doesn't look human, isn't human. I still say, they're human by their own terms. I don't care what word you want to use, when you call something something, that's what it is."

"A rose by any other name?" sneered Geoghan. "What about that? If you called it a cabbage would it smell like a cabbage?"

"It would be a rose-smelling cabbage," retorted Loesser.

"Why don't you call it off?" a voice put in. "You're both right and wrong at the same time, only you're too warped-in to see it?"

It was Chief Cadet Radetsky. In a service which was notorious for catching people young, he had already seen two years of active duty as an Ordinary Spaceman, and among his peers he was old – edging 19. He lounged in his chair, one leg thrown over the arm, his pale, sharp-featured face amused, but in spite of the laziness of his voice there was such a note of authority in it that the two fell silent.

"You don't agree, do you?" he went on. "That's ayo – just what I'd expect of a couple of grundies who've never been any farther than Marsport. Just the same, a thing can both be what you call it and not what you call it – and that's even more true in Far Out than it is here."

"The master has spoken," growled Geoghan. "Just because you've been around some –"

Radetsky sat up. "Ever been to Garfinkel III?"

"I never even heard of it," said Loesser, as Geoghan shook his head.

"I'm not surprised. Only two ships have been there, and I was on the second one. What's more, I'm the only human who's ever met a charging vargelvart and lived to tell about it."

A circle of silence had begun to spread from that centre. Someone said, "When was this?" and someone else said, "What's a vargelvart?"

"Ayo," said Radetsky. "If somebody'll find the bar in all this mess and order me a nullgrav splashed down, I'll tell you."

People began settling again in their chairs, or on table tops, and the tall, space-cold glass was passed from hand to hand until it got to him.

He took a sip, and said, "It was two years ago, my last hop. I'd been an OS for two years, in ComCen as some of you know, and after that they put me in for officer's training."

People nodded. It was common knowledge that Radetsky had done the three-year course in two years and would graduate in a couple of weeks.

"We didn't have much graph on Garfinkel III," he went on. "The first expedition came back with worms. Sounds crazy, but it's true – they picked up some kind of parasite like a tapeworm, and it gave them cramps and crazy visions, all that stuff. Almost wrecked the return trip. However, they had the worms inside them and the medics were able to develop an antidote so the next expedition would be safe.

"We landed on the same spot as Number One, near a big village where they'd made friends. At that time, nobody knew about the underworld civilization of the southern hemisphere. This village was on the fringe of the jungle, and the Commander set up a camp, re-established contact with the Ghavash, and we started our regular collecting and studying and all the rest of it. Ayo, well, I hate to admit it but in the very first week I got lost.

"It was a real grundy thing to do, almost as bad as the original. But remember, I was just a kid, I was 16."

Some 16-year-olds exchanged sour looks. Older people chuckled, remembering Admiral Abe Grundy who had mislaid a whole fleet of interstellar vessels during a reconnaissance.

"What happened," Radetsky said, "was that I was told to take another tri-comp set from the ship to the camp. I started out – it wasn't more than a quarter of a mile – and passed a clump of pretty flowers, or what looked like flowers, and went to look at them, and went a little farther, and a little farther, and the next thing – well, I don't know if you've ever seen real jungle – ('Are you kidding?' said Vieira, who came from Brazil) – but in ten minutes I couldn't find my way back and didn't know where I was, to find my way back from.

"There were thick-stemmed trees, their tops tangled so you couldn't see the sky, and vines climbing over them. Between them were things like fingers poking up through the ground, but covered with flower clusters. And the colours! They were what made me even more confused; there were colours you couldn't begin to guess at, like some crazy jigsaw puzzle scattered all over the table so you couldn't make sense of it. The ground was open enough in places so you could walk, all right, but the undergrowth was dense enough so you couldn't see far enough to get your bearings.

"Well, the first thing I did was sit down and take stock. I had the tri-comp set, which was great for instant surveying but didn't do me any good for finding my way back. It was heavy, too, and right then I decided I wasn't going to carry it around with me. I had a box of immunization pills – we had to take one a day – and some pop-skull gum, and a half-dozen dry ration bars because I had a hollow belly in those days, and liked my munchies. I had a knife, and a pistol on my belt, a Retlow .18, one of those little things like a toy but it carried plenty of punch; we had to wear them all the time, of course. However, I didn't have any ammunition except the ten shots in the clip. And that was about it.

"I tried to think about the things you're supposed to do when you're lost. Look for moss on the north sides of trees? There wasn't any moss, to start with."

"Why didn't you fire a couple of shots so they'd hear the noise?" asked Geoghan.

"Didn't you fire the Retlow in training?" Radetsky said, raising an eyebrow at him. "It makes a noise like somebody breaking a piece of spaghetti."

"You're supposed to just sit still when you're lost and wait for somebody to come and find you," said Vieira, primly.

"Uh-huh. I thought about that, too, and then I thought about something else finding me. Something hungry. I thought about the vargelvart, and decided I didn't want one of them to find me.

"We didn't know much about the vargelvart, or even much about that jungle, then. The first expedition had been too sick and too quick to learn much. We'd seen a few projections of local animals, and we knew a little more from the Ghavash. They didn't seem worried about anything except the vargelvart. They had a carving of one over the door of one of their houses, and I'd seen it – it wasn't a very big carving, but you got the idea all right of something big and solid and heavy. It had fan-shaped ears, four thick legs, a long curving snout —"

"An elephant!" said Loesser.

"Right. A kind of elephant, except with jagged meat-eating teeth and a long tail and sharp, wicked-looking horns. When the Ghavash talked about it they put their hands over their ears and made horrible faces, and said loudly 'Vareg!', which means fear. My boss, the Chief Communications Officer, told me the word vargelvart meant 'Fear Shouter'.

"Ayo, you can understand I didn't want to be stuck like a bug on one of those horns, or squashed under those feet. I figured I'd be better off walking and on my guard, so I could climb a tree or get behind one.

"Well, I was pretty sure I wasn't too far from the village. I didn't think I'd walked all that long. And I could remember that when I'd set out the sun had been at my back, and it was late morning so I figured I'd gone west. I could see the direction of the sunbeams poking down through the leaves, and I decided I'd try walking eastwards for a while and then, if I didn't get back, I'd build a smudge fire. Like most kids, I was oontsy; I didn't want the Commander to find me if I could find myself.

"So I started off. I walked for a long time, and it got to me after a while that the sun was right overhead and I didn't know which way I was walking. So I thought I'd better make a fire.

"By that time, I was in among some tall, smooth trees that looked like overgrown asparagus. Some of the branches had fallen but they were too big to burn. There were some bushes nearby but they had a tough, springy wood and I couldn't get my knife into it. I went on for a way and got in among some other kinds of trees and raked up some dry leaves, but when I put my lighter to them they just went *puff*! and vanished.

"I started to get scared. I lost my head – stupid, but that's what can happen. I began running, yelling at the top of my voice, and then all of a sudden I burst through some tall, feathery grasses and found myself in a clearing and face to face with an animal.

"No, it wasn't the vargelvart. It was a thing about the size of a coffee table and about the same shape. Sort of squarish, with a leg at each corner, only covered with rusty-coloured scales. It had a round head stuck on one end, and a pair of round eyes like a toad's on top. It didn't look dangerous, but I was too wound-up to think. I pulled out the pistol and fired three shots into it.

"Well, not really into it. More *on to* it. They whined and skidded off those scales without leaving a scratch.

"Before I could run, the thing was right in front of me. I remember saying 'Good doggy, good doggy'. It opened its mouth and out came a long, wide ribbon of tongue. It took hold of my pistol and pulled it out of my hand. The tongue went back in the mouth and I swear it smacked its lips.

"I just gawped at it. The tongue came out again and got hold of the metal strap of my wrist-watch and tried to take it off my wrist, and at that point I got my legs back and ran.

"I spent that night in a tree. In the morning, I climbed to the top of it and tried to spot the hull of the ship, or smoke, or anything, but there was nothing but tree-tops. I climbed down and started off eastwards, as near as I could make it.

"I don't even want to think about the next two days. That's right, two days of climbing, wandering, slopping through a marsh where I saw some nasty-looking lizards but they didn't bother me, crashing through thickets with long hairy spikes that broke off in your skin and itched like mad, and fighting off flying bugs that crawled all over me and nearly drove me wild but didn't sting, anyway, so there was something to be thankful for. And all the time I thought about the vargelvart. I didn't have any weapon but my knife. I thought about making a flint-headed spear, but I didn't know what flint looked like, and I thought some more about fighting an elephant with a stick and decided it would be a waste of time. But I cut a thick sapling for a club so I could defend myself against anything else that was smaller.

"The only lucky thing was that there was plenty of water, just plain old water, lots of little streams, so even though I didn't have anything left to eat by the third day, I got by. You can go for a long time without food if you have to, but not without water. By the morning of the fourth day I was a mess. I was weak and stinking and ragged and starving, and as miserable as a cat in a bog.

"That morning, I staggered up a little rocky hill. It was open on top, no trees, and I thought I'd just sit there and wait for something to happen. When I got to the top, I was looking out over the jungle. It spread around me on three sides, but down in front of me there was just brush, and then a stretch of brown plain. Far off, on the edge of the trees on the right I could see regular shapes and among the green and grey and brown I could make out the glint of metal. It was the ship and the roofs of the village. I had walked in a big semi-circle right away from them and through that whole damn jungle, and all I had to do was climb down and cut across the open plain and skirt the jungle and I'd be back. Maybe it would take half a day.

"That gave me the strength I needed. I somehow got down the face of the hill, and started through the brush. I had the jungle on my right, you know, and I sat down for a minute to get my head together. And then I heard a sound that froze me as solid as one of Jupiter's moons. I don't know how to describe it. Maybe something between a roar and a scream. It wasn't like an animal at all, it curdled up your blood like sour milk, it sounded like somebody being torn apart, or somebody in hell. God! Just remembering it is enough to make my belly cold.

"It couldn't have been anything but the Fear Shouter.

"I jumped up. I was out in the open, nothing but low bushes around me, the nearest tree was in the jungle, and that's where the sound was coming from. I had that rotten little stick and my knife, and I didn't have strength enough to run.

"Then, there it was, before I could do anything anyway. It came out from between the trees, its trunk raised, its little piggy eyes red, its fangs bared. It lowered its head so that sharp horns pointed at me, and charged."

He stopped, and wiped his forehead on his sleeve.

Loesser said, "You're kidding, aren't you? Is this all true?"

"Are you saying I'm a liar?" Radetsky asked coldly.

"Well – um – no," Loesser replied. "But how could you escape? How'd you get away? It's impossible!"

"No it's not," said Radetsky. "It's just a matter of what you and Geoghan were talking about before, what started the whole discussion – a thing being called what you call it and not what you call it."

"You mean the Fear Shouter wasn't a kind of elephant?" Geoghan demanded.

"Oh, yes, it was a kind of elephant, all right," said Radetsky. "But it was only about a foot high."

There was a moment of silence. Then Loesser said, "Then what'd you mean when you said you were the only human to meet a charging vargelvart and lived to tell about it? Other people must have seen them since."

"I don't think so," Radetsky said, rather wistfully. "They were terribly rare – that one may have been the last. You see, the Ghavash found them absolutely delicious. And so did I."

The Wind from the Sun

Arthur C. Clarke

THE ENORMOUS DISC of sail strained at its rigging, already filled with the wind that blew between the worlds. In three minutes the race would begin, yet now John Merton felt more relaxed, more at peace, than at any time for the past year. Whatever happened when the Commodore gave the starting signal, whether *Diana* carried him to victory or defeat, he had achieved his ambition. After a lifetime spent designing ships for others, now he would sail his own.

"T minus two minutes," said the cabin radio. "Please confirm your readiness."

One by one, the other skippers answered. Merton recognized all the voices – some tense, some calm – for they were the voices of his friends and rivals. On the four inhabited worlds, there were scarcely twenty men who could sail a sun yacht; and they were all here, on the starting line or aboard the escort vessels, orbiting twenty-two thousand miles above the equator.

"Number One – *Gossamer* – ready to go."

"Number Two – *Santa Maria* – all OK."

"Number Three – *Sunbeam* – OK."

"Number Four – *Woomera* – all systems go."

Merton smiled at that last echo from the early, primitive days of astronautics. But it had become part of the tradition of space; and there were times when a man needed to evoke the shades of those who had gone before him to the stars.

"Number Five – *Lebedev* – we're ready."

"Number Six – *Arachne* – OK."

Now it was his turn, at the end of the line; strange to think that the words he was speaking in this tiny cabin were being heard by at least five billion people.

"Number Seven – *Diana* – ready to start."

"One through Seven acknowledged," answered the impersonal voice from the judge's launch. "Now T minus one minute."

Merton scarcely heard it. For the last time, he was checking the tension in the rigging. The needles of all the dynamometers were steady; the immense sail was taut, its mirror surface sparkling and glittering gloriously in the sun.

To Merton, floating weightless at the periscope, it seemed to fill the sky. As well it might – for out there were fifty million square feet of sail, linked to his capsule by almost a hundred miles of rigging. All the canvas of all the tea clippers that had once raced like clouds across the China seas, sewn into one gigantic sheet, could not match the single sail that *Diana* had spread beneath the sun. Yet it was little more substantial than a soap bubble; that two square miles of aluminized plastic was only a few millionths of an inch thick.

"T minus ten seconds. All recording cameras ON."

Something so huge, yet so frail, was hard for the mind to grasp. And it was harder still to realize that this fragile mirror could tow him free of Earth merely by the power of the sunlight it would trap.

". . . five, four, three, two, one, CUT!"

Seven knife blades sliced through seven thin lines tethering the yachts to the mother ships that had assembled and serviced them. Until this moment, all had been circling the Earth together in a rigidly held formation, but now the yachts would begin to disperse, like dandelion seeds drifting before the breeze. And the winner would be the one that first drifted past the Moon.

Aboard *Diana*, nothing seemed to be happening. But Merton knew better. Though his body could feel no thrust, the instrument board told him that he was now accelerating at almost one-thousandth of a gravity. For a rocket, that figure would have been ludicrous – but this was the first time any solar yacht had ever attained it. *Diana*'s design was sound; the vast sail was living up to his calculations. At this rate, two circuits of the Earth would build up his speed to escape velocity, and then he could head out for the Moon, with the full force of the Sun behind him.

The full force of the Sun . . . He smiled wryly, remembering all his attempts to explain solar sailing to those lecture audiences back on Earth. That had been the only way he could raise money, in those early days. He might be Chief Designer of Cosmodyne Corporation, with a whole string of successful spaceships to his credit, but his firm had not been exactly enthusiastic about his hobby.

"Hold your hands out to the Sun," he'd said. "What do you feel? Heat, of course. But there's pressure as well – though you've never noticed it, because it's so tiny. Over the area of your hands, it comes to only about a millionth of an ounce.

"But out in space, even a pressure as small as that can be important, for it's acting all the time, hour after hour, day after day. Unlike rocket fuel, it's free and unlimited. If we want to, we can use it. We can build sails to catch the radiation blowing from the Sun."

At that point, he would pull out a few square yards of sail material and toss it towards the audience. The silvery film would coil and twist like smoke, then drift slowly to the ceiling in the hot-air currents.

"You can see how light it is," he'd continue. "A square mile weighs only a ton, and can collect five pounds of radiation pressure. So it will start moving – and we can let it tow us along, if we attach rigging to it.

"Of course, its acceleration will be tiny – about a thousandth of a g. That doesn't seem much, but let's see what it means.

"It means that in the first second, we'll move about a fifth of an inch. I suppose a healthy snail could do better than that. But after a minute, we've covered sixty feet, and will be doing just over a mile an hour. That's not bad, for something driven by pure sunlight! After an hour, we're forty miles from our starting point, and will be moving at eighty miles an hour. Please remember that in space there's no friction; so once you start anything moving, it will keep going forever. You'll be surprised when I tell you what our thousandth-of-a-g sailboat will be doing at the end of a day's run: *almost two thousand miles an hour*! If it starts from orbit – as it has to, of course – it can reach escape velocity in a couple of days. And all without burning a single drop of fuel!"

Well, he'd convinced them, and in the end he'd even convinced Cosmodyne. Over the last twenty years, a new sport had come into being. It had been called the sport of billionaires, and that was true. But it was beginning to pay for itself in terms of publicity and TV coverage. The prestige of four continents and two worlds was riding on this race, and it had the biggest audience in history.

Diana had made a good start; time to take a look at the opposition. Moving very gently – though there were shock absorbers between the control capsule and the delicate rigging, he was determined to run no risks – Merton stationed himself at the periscope.

There they were, looking like strange silver flowers painted in the dark fields of space. The nearest, South America's *Santa Maria*, was only fifty miles away; it bore a close resemblance to a boy's kite, but a kite more than a mile on a side. Farther away, the University of Astrograd's *Lebedev* looked like a Maltese cross; the sails that formed the four arms could apparently be tilted for steering purposes. In contrast, the Federation of Australasia's *Woomera* was a simple parachute, four miles in circumference. General Spacecraft's *Arachne*, as its name suggested, looked like a spider web, and had been built on the same principles, by robot shuttles spiralling out from a central point. Eurospace Corporation's *Gossamer* was an identical design, on a slightly smaller scale. And the Republic of Mars's *Sunbeam* was a flat ring, with a half-mile-wide hole in the centre, spinning slowly, so that centrifugal force gave it stiffness. That was an old idea, but no one had ever made it work; and Merton was fairly sure that the colonials would be in trouble when they started to turn.

That would not be for another six hours, when the yachts had moved along the first quarter of their slow and stately twenty-four-hour orbit. Here at the beginning of the race, they were all heading directly away from the Sun – running, as it were, before the solar wind. One had to make the most of this lap, before the boats swung around to the other side of the Earth and then started to head back into the Sun.

Time, Merton told himself, for the first check, while he had no navigational worries. With the periscope, he made a careful examination of the sail, concentrating on the points where the rigging was attached to it. The shroud lines – narrow bands of unsilvered plastic film – would have been completely invisible had they not been coated with fluorescent paint. Now they were taut lines of coloured light, dwindling away for hundreds of yards towards that gigantic sail. Each had its own electric windlass, not much bigger than a game fisherman's reel. The little windlasses were continually turning, playing lines in or out as the autopilot kept the sail trimmed at the correct angle to the Sun.

The play of sunlight on the great flexible mirror was

beautiful to watch. The sail was undulating in slow, stately oscillations, sending multiple images of the Sun marching across it, until they faded away at its edges. Such leisurely vibrations were to be expected in this vast and flimsy structure. They were usually quite harmless, but Merton watched them carefully. Sometimes they could build up to the catastrophic undulations known as the 'wriggles', which could tear a sail to pieces.

When he was satisfied that everything was shipshape, he swept the periscope around the sky, rechecking the positions of his rivals. It was as he had hoped: the weeding-out process had begun, as the less efficient boats fell astern. But the real test would come when they passed into the shadow of Earth. Then, manoeuvrability would count as much as speed.

It seemed a strange thing to do, what with the race having just started, but he thought it might be a good idea to get some sleep. The two-man crews on the other boats could take it in turns, but Merton had no one to relieve him. He must rely on his own physical resources, like that other solitary seaman, Joshua Slocum, in his tiny *Spray*. The American skipper had sailed *Spray* singlehanded around the world; he could never have dreamed that, two centuries later, a man would be sailing singlehanded from Earth to Moon – inspired, at least partly, by his example.

Merton snapped the elastic bands of the cabin seat around his waist and legs, then placed the electrodes of the sleep-inducer on his forehead. He set the timer for three hours, and relaxed. Very gently, hypnotically, the electronic pulses throbbed in the frontal lobes of his brain. Coloured spirals of light expanded beneath his closed eyelids, widening outwards to infinity. Then nothing . . .

The brazen clamour of the alarm dragged him back from his dreamless sleep. He was instantly awake, his eyes scanning the instrument panel. Only two hours had passed – but above the accelerometer, a red light was flashing. Thrust was falling; *Diana* was losing power.

Merton's first thought was that something had happened to the sail; perhaps the antispin devices had failed, and the rigging had become twisted. Swiftly, he checked the meters that showed the tension of the shroud lines. Strange – on one side of the sail they were reading normally, but on the other the pull was dropping slowly, even as he watched.

In sudden understanding, Merton grabbed the periscope, switched to wide-angle vision, and started to scan the edge of the sail. Yes – there was the trouble, and it could have only one cause.

A huge, sharp-edged shadow had begun to slide across the gleaming silver of the sail. Darkness was falling upon *Diana*, as if a cloud had passed between her and the Sun. And in the dark, robbed of the rays that drove her, she would lose all thrust and drift helplessly through space.

But, of course, there were no clouds here more than twenty thousand miles above the Earth. If there was a shadow, it must be made by man.

Merton grinned as he swung the periscope towards the Sun, switching in the filters that would allow him to look full into its blazing face without being blinded.

"Manoeuvre 4a," he muttered to himself. "We'll see who can play best at *that* game."

It looked as if a giant planet was crossing the face of the Sun; a great black disc had bitten deep into its edge. Twenty miles astern, *Gossamer* was trying to arrange an artificial eclipse, specially for *Diana*'s benefit.

The manoeuvre was a perfectly legitimate one. Back in the days of ocean racing, skippers had often tried to rob each other of the wind. With any luck, you could leave your rival becalmed, with his sails collapsing around him – and be well ahead before he could undo the damage.

Merton had no intention of being caught so easily. There was plenty of time to take evasive action; things happened very slowly when you were running a solar sailboat. It would be at least twenty minutes before *Gossamer* could slide completely across the face of the Sun, and leave him in darkness.

Diana's tiny computer – the size of a matchbox, but the equivalent of a thousand human mathematicians – considered the problem for a full second and then flashed the answer. He'd have to open control panels three and four, until the sail had developed an extra twenty degrees of tilt; then the radiation pressure would blow him out of *Gossamer*'s dangerous shadow, back into the full blast of the Sun. It was a pity to interfere with the autopilot, which had been carefully programmed to give the fastest possible run – but that, after all, was why he was here. This was what made solar yachting a sport, rather than a battle between computers.

Out went control lines one and six, slowly undulating like sleepy snakes as they momentarily lost their tension. Two miles away, the triangular panels began to open lazily, spilling sunlight through the sail. Yet, for a long time, nothing seemed to happen. It was hard to grow accustomed to this slow-moving world, where it took minutes for the effects of any action to become visible to the eye. Then Merton saw that the sail was indeed tipping towards the Sun – and that *Gossamer*'s shadow was sliding harmlessly away, its cone of darkness lost in the deeper night of space.

Long before the shadow had vanished, and the disc of the Sun had cleared again, he reversed the tilt and brought *Diana* back on course. Her new momentum would carry her clear of the danger; no need to overdo it, and upset his calculations by side-stepping too far. That was another rule that was hard to learn; the very moment you had started something happening in space, it was already time to think about stopping it.

He reset the alarm, ready for the next natural or manmade emergency. Perhaps *Gossamer* or one of the other contestants would try the same trick again. Meanwhile, it was time to eat, though he did not feel particularly hungry. One used little physical energy in space, and it was easy to forget about food. Easy – and dangerous; for when an emergency arose, you might not have the reserves to deal with it.

He broke open the first of the meal packets, and inspected it without enthusiasm. The name on the label –

SPACETASTIES – was enough to put him off. And he had grave doubts about the promise printed underneath: 'Guaranteed crumbless'. It had been said that crumbs were a greater danger to space vehicles than meteorites; they could drift into the most unlikely places, causing short-circuits, blocking vital jets, and getting into instruments that were supposed to be hermetically sealed.

Still, the liverwurst went down pleasantly enough; so did the chocolate and the pineapple purée. The plastic coffee bulb was warming on the electric heater when the outside world broke in upon his solitude, as the radio operator on the Commodore's launch routed a call to him.

"Dr Merton? If you can spare the time, Jeremy Blair would like a few words with you." Blair was one of the more responsible news commentators, and Merton had been on his programme many times. He could refuse to be interviewed, of course, but he liked Blair, and at the moment he certainly could not claim to be too busy. "I'll take it," he answered.

"Hello, Dr Merton," said the commentator immediately. "Glad you can spare a few minutes. And congratulations – you seem to be ahead of the field."

"Too early in the game to be sure of *that*," Merton answered cautiously.

"Tell me, Doctor, why did you decide to sail *Diana* by yourself? Just because it's never been done before?"

"Well, isn't that a good reason? But it wasn't the only one, of course." He paused, choosing his words carefully. "You know how critically the performance of a sun yacht depends on its mass. A second man, with all his supplies, would mean another five hundred pounds. That could easily be the difference between winning and losing."

"And you're quite certain that you can handle *Diana* alone?"

"Reasonably sure, thanks to the automatic controls I've designed. My main job is to supervise and make decisions."

"But – two square miles of sail! It just doesn't seem possible for one man to cope with all that."

Merton laughed. "Why not? Those two square miles produce a maximum pull of just ten pounds. I can exert more force with my little finger."

"Well, thank you, Doctor. And good luck. I'll be calling you again."

As the commentator signed off, Merton felt a little ashamed of himself. For his answers had been only part of the truth; and he was sure Blair was shrewd enough to know it.

There was just one reason why he was here, alone in space. For almost forty years he had worked with teams of hundreds or even thousands of men, helping to design the most complex vehicles that the world had ever seen. For the last twenty years he had led one of those teams, and watched his creations go soaring to the stars. (Sometimes . . . There *were* failures, which he could never forget, even though the fault had not been his.) He was famous, with a successful career behind him. Yet he had never done anything by himself; always he had been one of an army.

This was his last chance to try for individual achievement,

and he would share it with no one. There would be no more solar yachting for at least five years, as the period of the Quiet Sun ended and the cycle of bad weather began, with radiation storms bursting through the solar system. When it was safe again for these frail, unshielded craft to venture aloft, he would be too old. If, indeed, he was not too old already . . .

He dropped the empty food containers into the waste disposal and turned once more to the periscope. At first he could find only five of the other yachts; there was no sign of *Woomera*. It took him several minutes to locate her − a dim, star-eclipsing phantom, neatly caught in the shadow of *Lebedev*. He could imagine the frantic efforts the Australians were making to extricate themselves, and wondered how they had fallen into the trap. It suggested that *Lebedev* was unusually manoeuvrable. She would bear watching, though she was too far away to menace *Diana* at the moment.

Now the Earth had almost vanished; it had waned to a narrow, brilliant bow of light that was moving steadily towards the Sun. Dimly outlined within that burning bow was the night side of the planet, with the phosphorescent gleams of great cities showing here and there through gaps in the clouds. The disc of darkness had already blanked out a huge section of the Milky Way. In a few minutes, it would start to encroach upon the Sun.

The light was fading; a purple, twilight hue − the glow of many sunsets, thousands of miles below − was falling across the sail as *Diana* slipped silently into the shadow of Earth. The Sun plummeted below that invisible horizon; within minutes, it was night.

Merton looked back along the orbit he had traced, now a quarter of the way around the world. One by one he saw the brilliant stars of the other yachts wink out, as they joined him in the brief night. It would be an hour before the Sun emerged from that enormous black shield, and through all that time they would be completely helpless, coasting without power.

He switched on the external spotlight, and started to search the now-darkened sail with its beam. Already the thousands of acres of film were beginning to wrinkle and become flaccid. The shroud lines were slackening, and must be wound in lest they become entangled. But all this was expected; everything was going as planned.

Fifty miles astern, *Arachne* and *Santa Maria* were not so lucky. Merton learned of their troubles when the radio burst into life on the emergency circuit.

"Number Two and Number Six, this is Control. You are on a collision course; your orbits will intersect in sixty-five minutes! Do you require assistance?"

There was a long pause while the two skippers digested this bad news. Merton wondered who was to blame. Perhaps one yacht had been trying to shadow the other, and had not completed the manoeuvre before they were both caught in darkness. Now there was nothing that either could do. They were slowly but inexorably converging, unable to change course by a fraction of a degree.

Yet – sixty-five minutes! That would just bring them out

into sunlight again, as they emerged from the shadow of the Earth. They had a slim chance, if their sails could snatch enough power to avoid a crash. There must be some frantic calculations going on aboard *Arachne* and *Santa Maria*.

Arachne answered first. Her reply was just what Merton had expected.

"Number Six calling Control. We don't need assistance, thank you. We'll work this out for ourselves."

I wonder, thought Merton; *but at least it will be interesting to watch*. The first real drama of the race was approaching, exactly above the line of midnight on the sleeping Earth.

For the next hour, Merton's own sail kept him too busy to worry about *Arachne* and *Santa Maria*. It was hard to keep a good watch on that fifty million square feet of dim plastic out there in the darkness, illuminated only by his narrow spotlight and the rays of the still-distant Moon. From now on, for almost half his orbit around the Earth, he must keep the whole of this immense area edge-on to the Sun. During the next twelve or fourteen hours, the sail would be a useless encumbrance; for he would be heading *into* the Sun, and its rays could only drive him backwards along his orbit. It was a pity that he could not furl the sail completely, until he was ready to use it again; but no one had yet found a practical way of doing this.

Far below, there was the first hint of dawn along the edge of the Earth. In ten minutes the Sun would emerge from its eclipse. The coasting yachts would come to life again as the blast of radiation struck their sails. That would be the moment of crisis for *Arachne* and *Santa Maria* – and, indeed, for all of them.

Merton swung the periscope until he found the two dark shadows drifting against the stars. They were very close together – perhaps less than three miles apart. They might, he decided, just be able to make it . . .

Dawn flashed like an explosion along the rim of Earth as the Sun rose out of the Pacific. The sail and shroud lines glowed a brief crimson, then gold, then blazed with the pure white light of day. The needles of the dynamometers began to lift from their zeroes – but only just. *Diana* was still almost completely weightless, for with the sail pointing towards the Sun, her acceleration was now only a few millionths of a gravity.

But *Arachne* and *Santa Maria* were crowding on all the sail that they could manage, in their desperate attempt to keep apart. Now, while there was less than two miles between them, their glittering plastic clouds were unfurling and expanding with agonizing slowness as they felt the first delicate push of the Sun's rays. Almost every TV screen on Earth would be mirroring this protracted drama; and even now, at this last minute, it was impossible to tell what the outcome would be.

The two skippers were stubborn men. Either could have cut his sail and fallen back to give the other a chance; but neither would do so. Too much prestige, too many millions, too many reputations were at stake. And so, silently and softly as snowflakes falling on a winter night, *Arachne* and *Santa*

Maria collided.

The square kite crawled almost imperceptibly into the circular spider web. The long ribbons of the shroud lines twisted and tangled together with dreamlike slowness. Even aboard *Diana*, Merton, busy with his own rigging, could scarcely tear his eyes away from this silent, long-drawn-out disaster.

For more than ten minutes the billowing, shining clouds continued to merge into one inextricable mass. Then the crew capsules tore loose and went their separate ways, missing each other by hundreds of yards. With a flare of rockets, the safety launches hurried to pick them up.

That leaves five of us, thought Merton. He felt sorry for the skippers who had so thoroughly eliminated each other, only a few hours after the start of the race, but they were young men and would have another chance.

Within minutes, the five had dropped to four. From the beginning, Merton had had doubts about the slowly rotating *Sunbeam*; now he saw them justified.

The Martian ship had failed to tack properly. Her spin had given her too much stability. Her great ring of a sail was turning to face the Sun, instead of being edge-on to it. She was being blown back along her course at almost her maximum acceleration.

That was about the most maddening thing that could happen to a skipper – even worse than a collision, for he could blame only himself. But no one would feel much sympathy for the frustrated colonials, as they dwindled slowly astern. They had made too many brash boasts before the race, and what had happened to them was poetic justice.

Yet it would not do to write off *Sunbeam* completely; with almost half a million miles still to go, she might yet pull ahead. Indeed, if there were a few more casualties, she might be the only one to complete the race. It had happened before.

The next twelve hours were uneventful, as the Earth waxed in the sky from new to full. There was little to do while the fleet drifted around the unpowered half of its orbit, but Merton did not find the time hanging heavily on his hands. He caught a few hours of sleep, ate two meals, wrote his log, and became involved in several more radio interviews. Sometimes, though rarely, he talked to the other skippers, exchanging greetings and friendly taunts. But most of the time he was content to float in weightless relaxation, beyond all the cares of Earth, happier than he had been for many years. He was – as far as any man could be in space – master of his own fate, sailing the ship upon which he had lavished so much skill, so much love, that it had become part of his very being.

The next casualty came when they were passing the line between Earth and Sun, and were just beginning the powered half of the orbit. Aboard *Diana*, Merton saw the great sail stiffen as it tilted to catch the rays that drove it. The acceleration began to climb up from the microgravities, though it would be hours yet before it would reach its maximum value.

It would never reach it for *Gossamer*. The moment when

power came on again was always critical, and she failed to survive it.

Blair's radio commentary, which Merton had left running at low volume, alerted him with the news: "Hello, *Gossamer* has the wriggles!" He hurried to the periscope, but at first could see nothing wrong with the great circular disc of *Gossamer's* sail. It was difficult to study it because it was almost edge-on to him and so appeared as a thin ellipse; but presently he saw that it was twisting back and forth in slow, irresistible oscillations. Unless the crew could damp out these waves, by properly timed but gentle tugs on the shroud lines, the sail would tear itself to pieces.

They did their best, and after twenty minutes it seemed that they had succeeded. Then, somewhere near the centre of the sail, the plastic film began to rip. It was slowly driven outwards by the radiation pressure, like smoke coiling upwards from a fire. Within a quarter of an hour, nothing was left but the delicate tracery of the radial spars that had supported the great web. Once again there was a flare of rockets, as a launch moved in to retrieve the *Gossamer's* capsule and her dejected crew.

"Getting rather lonely up here, isn't it?" said a conversational voice over the ship-to-ship radio.

"Not for you, Dimitri," retorted Merton. "You've still got company back there at the end of the field. I'm the one who's lonely, up here in front." It was not an idle boast; by this time *Diana* was three hundred miles ahead of the next competitor, and her lead should increase still more rapidly in the hours to come.

Aboard *Lebedev*, Dimitri Markoff gave a good-natured chuckle. He did not sound, Merton thought, at all like a man who had resigned himself to defeat.

"Remember the legend of the tortoise and the hare," answered the Russian. "A lot can happen in the next quarter-million miles."

It happened much sooner than that, when they had completed their first orbit of Earth and were passing the starting line again – though thousands of miles higher, thanks to the extra energy the Sun's rays had given them. Merton had taken careful sights on the other yachts, and had fed the figures into the computer. The answer it gave for *Woomera* was so absurd that he immediately did a recheck.

There was no doubt about it – the Australasians were catching up at a completely fantastic rate. No solar yacht could possibly have such an acceleration, unless . . .

A swift look through the periscope gave the answer. *Woomera*'s rigging, pared back to the very minimum of mass, had given way. It was her sail alone, still maintaining its shape, that was racing up behind him like a handkerchief blown before the wind. Two hours later it fluttered past, less than twenty miles away; but long before that, the Australasians had joined the growing crowd aboard the Commodore's launch.

So now it was a straight fight between *Diana* and *Lebedev* – for though the Martians had not given up, they were a thousand miles astern and no longer counted as a serious threat. For that matter, it was hard to see what *Lebedev* could do to overtake *Diana's* lead; but all the way around the second lap, through eclipse again and the long, slow drift against the Sun, Merton felt a growing unease.

He knew the Russian pilots and designers. They had been trying to win this race for twenty years – and, after all, it was only fair that they should, for had not Pyotr Nikolaevich Lebedev been the first man to detect the pressure of sunlight, back at the very beginning of the twentieth century? But they had never succeeded.

And they would never stop trying. Dimitri was up to something – and it would be spectacular.

Aboard the official launch, a thousand miles behind the racing yachts, Commodore van Stratten looked at the radiogram with angry dismay. It had travelled more than a hundred million miles, from the chain of solar observatories swinging high above the blazing surface of the Sun; and it brought the worst possible news.

The Commodore – his title was purely honorary, of course; back on Earth he was Professor of Astrophysics at Harvard – had been half expecting it. Never before had the race been arranged so late in the season. There had been, many delays; they had gambled – and now, it seemed, they might all lose.

Deep beneath the surface of the Sun, enormous forces were gathering. At any moment the energies of a million hydrogen bombs might burst forth in the awesome explosion known as a solar flare. Climbing at millions of miles an hour, an invisible fireball many times the size of Earth would leap from the Sun and head out across space.

The cloud of electrified gas would probably miss the Earth completely. But if it did not, it would arrive in just over a day. Spaceships could protect themselves, with their shielding and their powerful magnetic screens; but the lightly built solar yachts, with their paper-thin walls, were defenceless against such a menace. The crews would have to be taken off, and the race abandoned.

John Merton knew nothing of this as he brought *Diana* around the Earth for the second time. If all went well, this would be the last circuit, both for him and for the Russians. They had spiralled upwards by thousands of miles, gaining energy from the Sun's rays. On this lap, they should escape from Earth completely, and head outwards on the long run to the Moon. It was a straight race now; *Sunbeam*'s crew had finally withdrawn exhausted, after battling valiantly with their spinning sail for more than a hundred thousand miles.

Merton did not feel tired; he had eaten and slept well, and *Diana* was behaving herself admirably. The autopilot, tensioning the rigging like a busy little spider, kept the great sail trimmed to the Sun more accurately than any human skipper could have. Though by this time the two square miles of plastic sheet must have been riddled by hundreds of micrometeorites, the pinhead-sized punctures had produced no falling off of thrust.

He had only two worries. The first was shroud line number eight, which could no longer be adjusted properly. Without any warning, the reel had jammed; even after all these years of astronautical engineering, bearings sometimes seized up in vacuum. He could neither lengthen nor shorten the line, and would have to navigate as best he could with the others. Luckily, the most difficult manoeuvres were over; from now on, *Diana* would have the Sun behind her as she sailed straight down the solar wind. And as the old-time sailors had often said, it was easy to handle a boat when the wind was blowing over your shoulder.

His other worry was *Lebedev*, still dogging his heels three hundred miles astern. The Russian yacht had shown remarkable manoeuvrability, thanks to the four great panels that could be tilted around the central sail. Her flipovers as she rounded the Earth had been carried out with superb precision. But to gain manoeuvrability she must have sacrificed speed. You could not have it both ways; in the long, straight haul ahead, Merton should be able to hold his own. Yet he could not be certain of victory until, three or four days from now, *Diana* went flashing past the side of the Moon.

And then, in the fiftieth hour of the race, just after the end of the second orbit around Earth, Markoff sprang his little surprise.

"Hello, John," he said casually over the ship-to-ship circuit. "I'd like you to watch this. It should be interesting."

Merton drew himself across to the periscope and turned up the magnification to the limit. There in the field of view, a most improbable sight against the background of the stars, was the glittering Maltese cross of *Lebedev*, very small but very clear. As he watched, the four arms of the cross slowly detached themselves from the central square, and went drifting away, with all their spars and rigging, into space.

Markoff had jettisoned all unnecessary mass, now that he was coming up to escape velocity and need no longer plod patiently around the Earth, gaining momentum on each circuit. From now on, *Lebedev* would be almost unsteerable – but that did not matter; all the tricky navigation lay behind her. It was as if an old-time yachtsman had deliberately thrown away his rudder and heavy keel, knowing that the rest of the race would be straight downwind over a calm sea.

"Congratulations, Dimitri," Merton radioed. "It's a neat trick. But it's not good enough. You can't catch up with me now."

"I've not finished yet," the Russian answered. "There's an old winter's tale in my country about a sleigh being chased by wolves. To save himself, the driver has to throw off the passengers one by one. Do you see the analogy?"

Merton did, all too well. On this final straight lap, Dimitri no longer needed his co-pilot. *Lebedev* could really be stripped down for action.

"Alexis won't be very happy about this," Merton replied. "Besides, it's against the rules."

"Alexis isn't happy, but I'm the captain. He'll just have to wait around for ten minutes until the Commodore picks him up. And the regulations say nothing about the size of the crew – *you* should know that."

Merton did not answer; he was too busy doing some hurried calculations, based on what he knew of *Lebedev*'s design. By the time he had finished, he knew that the race was still in doubt. *Lebedev* would be catching up with him at just about the time he hoped to pass the Moon.

But the outcome of the race was already being decided, ninety-two million miles away.

On Solar Observatory Three, far inside the orbit of Mercury, the automatic instruments recorded the whole history of the flare. A hundred million square miles of the Sun's surface exploded in such blue-white fury that, by comparison, the rest of the disc paled to a dull glow. Out of that seething inferno, twisting and turning like a living creature in the magnetic fields of its own creation, soared the electrified plasma of the great flare. Ahead of it, moving at the speed of light, went the warning flash of ultraviolet and X-rays. That would reach Earth in eight minutes, and was relatively harmless. Not so the charged atoms that were following behind at their leisurely four million miles an hour – and which, in just over a day, would engulf *Diana*, *Lebedev*, and their accompanying little fleet in a cloud of lethal radiation.

The Commodore left his decision to the last possible minute. Even when the jet of plasma had been tracked past the orbit of Venus, there was a chance that it might miss the Earth. But when it was less than four hours away, and had already been picked up by the Moon-based radar network, he knew that there was no hope. All solar sailing was over, for the next five or six years – until the Sun was quiet again.

A great sigh of disappointment swept across the solar

system. *Diana* and *Lebedev* were halfway between Earth and Moon, running neck and neck – and now no one would ever know which was the better boat. The enthusiasts would argue the result for years; history would merely record: "Race cancelled owing to solar storm."

When John Merton received the order, he felt a bitterness he had not known since childhood. Across the years, sharp and clear, came the memory of his tenth birthday. He had been promised an exact scale model of the famous spaceship *Morning Star*, and for weeks had been planning how he would assemble it, where he would hang it in his bedroom. And then, at the last moment, his father had broken the news. "I'm sorry, John – it cost too much money. Maybe next year . . ."

Half a century and a successful lifetime later, he was a heartbroken boy again.

For a moment, he thought of disobeying the Commodore. Suppose he sailed on, ignoring the warning? Even if the race was abandoned, he could make a crossing to the Moon that would stand in the record books for generations.

But that would be worse than stupidity; it would be suicide – and a very unpleasant form of suicide. He had seen men die of radiation poisoning, when the magnetic shielding of their ships had failed in deep space. No – nothing was worth that . . .

He felt as sorry for Dimitri Markoff as for himself. They had both deserved to win, and now victory would go to neither. No man could argue with the Sun in one of its rages, even though he might ride upon its beams to the edge of space.

Only fifty miles astern now, the Commodore's launch was drawing alongside *Lebedev*, preparing to take off her skipper. There went the silver sail, as Dimitri – with feelings that he would share – cut the rigging. The tiny capsule would be taken back to Earth, perhaps to be used again; but a sail was spread for one voyage only.

He could press the jettison button now, and save his rescuers a few minutes of time. But he could not do it; he wanted to stay aboard to the very end, on the little boat that had been for so long a part of his dreams and his life. The great sail was spread now at right angles to the Sun, exerting its utmost thrust. Long ago it had torn him clear of Earth, and *Diana* was still gaining speed.

Then, out of nowhere, beyond all doubt or hesitation, he knew what must be done. For the last time, he sat down before the computer that had navigated him halfway to the Moon.

When he had finished, he packed the log and his few personal belongings. Clumsily, for he was out of practice, and it was not an easy job to do by oneself, he climbed into the emergency survival suit. He was just sealing the helmet when the Commodore's voice called over the radio.

"We'll be alongside in five minutes, Captain. Please cut your sail, so we won't foul it."

John Merton, first and last skipper of the sun yacht *Diana*, hesitated a moment. He looked for the last time around the tiny cabin, with its shining instruments and its neatly arranged controls, now all locked in their final positions. Then he said into the microphone, "I'm abandoning ship. Take your time to pick me up. *Diana* can look after herself."

There was no reply from the Commodore, and for that he was grateful. Professor van Stratten would have guessed what was happening – and would know that, in these final moments, he wished to be left alone.

He did not bother to exhaust the airlock, and the rush of escaping gas blew him gently out into space. The thrust he gave her then was his last gift to *Diana*. She dwindled away from him, sail glittering splendidly in the sunlight that would be hers for centuries to come. Two days from now she would flash past the Moon; but the Moon, like the Earth, could never catch her. Without his mass to slow her down, she would gain two thousand miles an hour in every day of sailing. In a month, she would be travelling faster than any ship that man had ever built.

As the Sun's rays weakened with distance, so her acceleration would fall. But even at the orbit of Mars, she would be gaining a thousand miles an hour in every day. Long before then, she would be moving too swiftly for the Sun itself to hold her. Faster than a comet had ever streaked in from the stars, she would be heading out into the abyss.

The glare of rockets, only a few miles away, caught Merton's eye. The launch was approaching to pick him up – at thousands of times the acceleration that *Diana* could ever attain. But its engines could burn for a few minutes only, before they exhausted their fuel – while *Diana* would still be gaining speed, driven outwards by the Sun's eternal fires, for ages yet to come.

"Good-bye, little ship," said John Merton. "I wonder what eyes will see you next, how many thousand years from now?"

At last he felt at peace, as the blunt torpedo of the launch nosed up beside him. He would never win the race to the Moon; but his would be the first of all man's ships to set sail on the long journey to the stars.

ACKNOWLEDGEMENTS

For permission to reproduce copyright material, acknowledgement and thanks are due to the following: Laura Cecil Literary Agent for 'The Boy, the Dog and the Spaceship' © 1974 Nicholas Fisk, published from *Living Fire and Other Sci-Fi Stories* (Corgi); A P Watt Ltd for an extract from *The Invisible Man* by H G Wells; Houghton Mifflin Co for an extract from *A Wizard of Earthsea* by Ursula K. Le Guin. Copyright © 1968 by Ursula K. Le Guin. A Parnassus Press Book; MBA Literary Agents for 'Bobo's Star' © Glenn Chandler 1979; Jonathan Cape Ltd for an extract from *The Master* by T. H. White; MBA Literary Agents for 'The Specimen' © Tim Stout 1979; John Christopher for 'Of Polymuf Stock' and an extract from *The White Mountains* (part of the Tripods trilogy); Hamish Hamilton for an extract from *Crisis on Conshelf Ten* by Monica Hughes; Doubleday, a division of Bantam, Doubleday, Dell Publishing Group, Inc for 'The Fun They Had' from *Earth is Room Enough* by Isaac Asimov. Copyright © 1955 by King-Size Publications, Inc; The Estate of M. P. Sheil for 'The Last Man Alive' from *The Purple Cloud*; William Heinemann Ltd for an extract from *The War of the Worlds* by H. G. Wells; Abner Stein for 'All Summer in a Day' © 1954 by Ray Bradbury; renewed 1982 by Ray Bradbury; Michael Shaara for his story 'Grenville's Planet'; The Estate of Jay Williams for 'The Fear Shouter' by Jay Williams from *Unearthly Beasts and Other Strange People*; Arthur C. Clarke for 'The Wind from the Sun' from *Constellations: Stories of the Future* published by Victor Gollancz Ltd.

While every effort has been made to obtain permission, there may still be cases in which we have failed to trace a copyright holder, and we would like to apologize for any apparent negligence.